Fergus Hume

The Year of Miracle

A tale of the year one thousand nine hundred

Fergus Hume

The Year of Miracle
A tale of the year one thousand nine hundred

ISBN/EAN: 9783337174149

Printed in Europe, USA, Canada, Australia, Japan

Cover: Foto ©Andreas Hilbeck / pixelio.de

More available books at **www.hansebooks.com**

THE YEAR OF MIRACLE

A Tale of the Year One Thousand Nine Hundred

BY

FERGUS HUME

AUTHOR OF "THE MYSTERY OF A HANSOM CAB," "MADAME MIDAS,"
"MONSIEUR JUDAS," ETC.

"The breath of Heaven is the sword that slays"

COPYRIGHT

LONDON:

GEORGE ROUTLEDGE AND SONS, LIMITED

BROADWAY HOUSE, LUDGATE HILL

CONTENTS.

THE YEAR OF MIRACLE.

CHAPTER I.

A STRUGGLE-FOR-LIFER.

THE door was that of a respectable-looking house in Weymouth Street, in the year one thousand nine hundred, and
the bright, new brass plate attached to the door of the
respectable-looking house, displayed the name "Dr. Francis
Rebelspear," engraved in fat, black letters, defiantly prominent in their determination to attract the attention of the
public. Poor Rebelspear, he was very proud when he first
obtained the right to use that title, looking upon it as a
sure lure to those who desired to be cured by the applica-
tion of the latest medical science ; but, evidently, the sick,
the halt, the lame, and the blind—or rather the half-blind—
mistrusted the inexperienced look of that new brass plate,
for they invariably passed by on their way to some older
practitioner, while Dr. Francis sat gloomily in his empty
consulting-room, wondering when his turn would come to
experiment on the ailing bodies of his fellow-creatures.
The first brief, the first sermon, the first patient—it is all
very well to look back at them through the golden haze of

success, but it is not so pleasant to look forward to them with a lean purse and an anxious heart.

Rebelspear was anxious, terribly anxious, there was no doubt of that, for he had now been waiting many months for the incoming of patients, but as yet none had responded to the mute appeal of that brand-new brass plate which so eloquently declared the inexperience of its owner. After finishing his medical education, and obtaining his licence to kill or cure, he had found himself a fully qualified M.D. with comparatively little money at his disposal. The rent, rates, taxes, and furnishings of the respectable-looking house in Weymouth Street, the constant paying out and nothing coming in, had reduced that comparatively little to almost next to nothing; and as civilised man cannot live without a certain amount of capital, Dr. Rebelspear's future looked very gloomy indeed.

He was young—just turned thirty; he was clever—proved by sundry mystical letters tailing after his name; he was hopeful—*videlicet* the sprat-to-catch-a-mackerel house in Weymouth Street; but notwithstanding all these encouraging qualifications, it seemed as though this poor young man would be worsted in his encounter with the world. There were many, many doctors, and, as a compensatory law, there were many, many patients; but he was one of the many former, and these many latter did not come his way. So, as he could not forcibly drag them into his consulting-room, he had to sit there biting his nails and waiting—waiting for nothing, it appeared to him, unless it was the dawn of the twentieth century.

Here was a brilliant illustration of the Darwinian theory

concerning the survival of the fittest. Question : Was Rebelspear one of the fittest who would survive ? Answer : Entirely depends upon his capacity for holding out, or the public's giving in. At present, the public had evidently no intention of giving in, and Dr. Francis could certainly not hold out much longer, so matters were thus at a dead lock ; and, unless a miracle occurred—but then the age of miracles is past. Twentieth century—Materialism and a disbelief in the supernatural. Twentieth century—Dr. Rebelspear and a disbelief that he would ever succeed. An overcrowded profession, and Frank Rebelspear one of the crowd. A young doctor—a comparative pauper—a struggle-for-lifer, was there any chance of sending the ball rolling towards the Temple of Plutus by securing that important first patient ? Well, unless a miracle !—again ! Pshaw ! the twentieth century and miracles indeed. Fire and water were a better mixture.

Nine o'clock, said the respectable, black marble timepiece in the consulting-room—nine o'clock on a June evening at the height of the London season, and three people filled the empty room—well, hardly three, seeing the third was immortal and invisible. Dr. Francis and his friend, Julian Delicker, present in the flesh, and at the door, the good fairy, Hope, pausing for a moment before finally leaving this unlucky house by the new brass-plated door. Hope, charming fairy who lightens the doleful hearts of poor humanity, looked at Rebelspear seated at his desk with his head on his hands and a dreary frown on his handsome face, and then looked at Julian Delicker, leaning against the mantelpiece, in strange contrast to his friend.

Julian Delicker, man-about-town, society butterfly, well-to-do idler, and old schoolfellow of Frank Rebelspear's, who had come to cheer him up, and offer his help, his personal influence, his advice, in fact, everything except his purse, which was what the poor young doctor most needed. Hope looked regretfully at his tableau of wealth and poverty—of Grasshopper and Ant—but no, that comparison is hardly correct, for this time the fable was reversed and Grasshopper had the best of it, while Ant, unfortunate Ant, was in difficulties of the most perplexing nature. Will not Hope, the good fairy, stay where she is so much needed? No, she will not. Hope needs some inducement to remain, a promise, a prospect, a belief, but without one of these encouragements she flies, fickle fairy that she is; and in this pitiful case she fled with a tear in her eye, being loath to leave the Weymouth Street house. Still finding no place in the heart of Rebelspear, she fled and left the worker to be consoled by the idler.

Tick! tick! tick! from the respectable, black marble clock on the mantelpiece, against which lounged Julian. Yes, that was certainly excellent advice, but who would trust a pauper, who positively could not conceal his deficiency of income? Still it was amusing, and the antique joke might cheer Rebelspear, so Julian translated the advice of the respectable clock to the desponding doctor.

"If things are so bad, you'll have to live on 'tick,' Frank, at least so the clock says."

Dr. Rebelspear lifted his aching head from his hands and looked angrily at the timepiece and the adviser.

"If you came here to use slang and make jokes," he said,

resentfully, " you had better go away as soon as you can. I'm in no humour for jesting."

" I came here to take you to Sir Luke Kernshaw's ball," replied Julian, coolly arranging the carnation in his button-hole—" that is, if you care to come. It will cheer you up a bit."

" Cheer me up !" echoed the doctor, with a dreary laugh. "What a Job's comforter you are, Julian. I have no money —I have no patients. I have no hope of things improving, : and yet you talk about my going to a ball to be cheered up --—ridiculous !"

" At all events you will see Eva Kernshaw there."

" Worse and worse ! To see the woman I love, and know that I cannot hope to make her my wife because of my position. How can you suggest such a Tantalus-like tor-ture, Delicker ?"

" Tantalus ! Tantalus ! Eh ? who was he ? Some Greek fellow, wasn't he ? Don't be classical, Frank. We had too much of that sort of thing at school. I don't care about it now."

" You don't care about anything, except yourself."

" And why not ? Number One is the greatest number."

" From a selfish point of view, I suppose it is," retorted the doctor, filling his pipe ; " but I won't go to Kernshaw's to be tortured by a sight of the unattainable, and as for you, my friend, you'd better clear out, or the scent of tobacco smoke will spoil your nice evening clothes."

" Don't be nasty, Frank," said Delicker, taking a seat. " I have come to you, as your old schoolfellow, to see what I can do for you."

"And, as I have told you before, you can do nothing, except break your leg and let me set it, or poison yourself and take the emetic I prescribe."

"*Après !*"

"Oh, *après*, you can trumpet my praises abroad as the best doctor you know, and all those brainless idiots you call your friends will come to me to be cured of their fancied ailments. I shall become a fashionable physician and get knighted. Eva will marry me, and from the splendid gloom of Harley Street Sir Francis and Lady Rebelspear will set forth to be presented at court."

Dr. Rebelspear spoke in a semi-jocular fashion, making a jest of his own poverty, but his laughter was very much akin to tears, and he hastily enveloped himself in thick clouds of tobacco smoke, lest Julian should see the nervous agitation of his face. Delicker, however, was not looking at his friend, nor even paying much attention to his grotesquely bitter speech, being quite absorbed in rolling a cigarette, which he did in a characteristically neat fashion.

"It's about half-past nine," he said at last, having lighted his roll of tobacco, "so if you intend coming to Kernshaw's dance, you'd better dress at once."

"I'm not going !"

"My dear old misanthrope, it will do you good. Sitting here waiting for mythical patients will only make you mope over your troubles; while if you come with me, you will have a chance of speaking to Eva Kernshaw, and—"

"What's the good?" interrupted Rebelspear savagely, "it's like showing a hungry man a dinner, and forbidding him to touch it. I adore Eva, and she loves me; but because I am poor and unknown, her purse-proud old father won't hear of an engagement between us. No! no! my dear would-be-comforter, Eva Kernshaw is reserved for wealthy young men like yourself, not for a poor devil like me, who has got nothing in this overcrowded world but his brains to recommend him."

"If that is meant for me, Rebelspear, you can set your mind at rest. I am not a marrying man ; and if I were, Eva Kernshaw is certainly not the woman I would choose for my wife. The other sister is the more charming of the two."

"Night?"

"Yes! You adore golden-haired Day ; I admire dark-browed Night ; but while you want to marry Eva, I don't want to marry anybody. Besides, Laura Kernshaw admires you."

"Nonsense!"

"Oh, yes, she does! Lucky man to be adored by two lovely women who have been painted by an R.A. as Day and Night. It's a reverse of the judgment of Paris, my friend. To whom will you give the golden apple of discord?"

"You are classical now," said Rebelspear, with a faint smile ; "but, indeed, you are mistaken. I love Eva, and she returns my love ; as for Miss Laura, I don't believe she ever gives a thought to me."

"Well, come to-night and we shall see."

Frank looked round the comfortable room, at the sombre row of medical books, at his study table, whereon lay a new number of the *Lancet* he wished to read, at the clock, at his friend, and finally shook his head.

"Don't tempt me, Julian.   I have work to do."

"Oh, nonsense.   You know quite enough to cure any
patient who comes, and as they don't come, why worry your
brains?"

"I must be prepared."

"Well, one night won't make much difference.   No
patient will come to-night."

"No! I suppose not," said Rebelspear, gloomily;
"humanity must be healthier than it used to be, or there
are too many doctors; but, certainly, I don't see much
chance of making a living."

"What a pity there can't be a jolly good old plague."

"Delicker!"

"Well! what do you look so horrified for? It would do
good in two ways.   Give you patients and kill off a large
number of the superfluous population.   The world is getting
overcrowded, and what with socialism, anarchy, war, famine,
and Heaven only knows what, it's a bad look-out for the
twentieth century."

"Possibly it is, but I don't see how your receipt would
improve matters."

"Don't you?" said Julian, with surprise; "my dear old
mole, if all the weak, the sick, and the revolutionary were
killed off, think of how much smoothe things would go.
There would be more elbow-room—more chance of humanity
developing.   We would rid ourselves of a criminal population—bread would not be so dear—there would be work for
all—in fact, the whole of this overcrowded planet we call
earth would make a fresh start, not as savages, but with all
the accumulated wisdom of centuries to begin with.   Under

these circumstances, think what a brilliant twentieth century we should have."

"How horribly paradoxical you are," replied Rebelspear, with a shudder. "You would sacrifice the many for the benefit of the few."

"Well, yes; if you like to put it that way. It would be a case of the survival of the fittest."

"No doubt; but think what a wonderfully discriminating plague would be necessary. To kill off all the criminals and spare the brainworkers. To put out of existence the lame and the deformed, in order to save the physically perfect. A most selective plague, truly."

"Oh, you may laugh as you please, Frank," said Julian, rather piqued, "but things are getting to such a pitch that unless we have a great war or a great plague everything will go to the devil."

"There is not much chance of the one or the other. Military weapons have been brought to such a pitch of perfection that each nation is afraid of the other, as a war in the present state of devilish ingenuity would mean the annihilation of one or the other; while, as for a plague, what with our recent discoveries in medical science, sickness on a large scale is not likely to occur. You can, therefore, my dear philanthropist, dismiss your *bizarre* idea of a plague as a regenerative measure for the humanity of the twentieth century, and—"

At this moment the servant entered with a grin on his face. "Please, sir, a patient!"

"A patient!" echoed Rebelspear, in a tone of disbelief.

"Shakespeare," cried Julian, with a gay laugh. "'There is a tide in the affairs of men—'"

"Oh, don't quote any more," said Frank, rising quickly. "I'll take this patient at the flood anyhow, and if it, or rather he, leads on to fortune—"

"Well?"

"I'll marry Eva Kernshaw."

CHAPTER II.

So that difficult first step had at last been taken, and Dr. Rebelspear had obtained his first patient. Certainly, when this long-expected and much-prized individual appeared, he did not look very promising, as, judging from his looks, he was not gifted with a superfluity of this world's goods. Still he was distinctly a patient—one who had come to ask the advice of the young doctor regarding his ailments, and that was something to be grateful for; so when the servant had departed and the prize was safely caged in the consulting-room, Rebelspear took a long, long look at this shabby old man, in order to assure himself that he was flesh and blood, and not a mere phantom creation of the brain.

Not that he looked unlike a phantom either, for he was very tall and very thin, while his black clothes hung round his bony frame in a loose fluttering fashion which gave him a wavering appearance. As he stood there in the strong electric light with his long white locks flowing over his shoulders, and his long white beard streaming down to his waist, both young men were struck by his unsubstantial look, which suggested all kinds of fanciful horrors.

11

But his eyes—ah, those terrible eyes! the light from which streamed out from under his frowning white eyebrows like the flash of gems—these gave a fierce, repellent look to his venerable face, a face lined and marked and scored and seamed with innumerable wrinkles betokening great age. His rounded shoulders were much bent, and with his thin, hooked nose, his long, claw-like fingers clutching his hat, and those brilliant eyes, he looked like some ill-omened bird of prey waiting to pounce on his victim.

Julian stared at this grotesquely terrible figure in his usual nonchalant manner, then, shrugging his shoulders, prepared to take his departure, when Rebelspear stopped him.

"Don't go, Delicker," he said, quickly, resuming his seat; "when I have finished with this gentleman I will go with you to Sir Luke Kernshaw's."

"Sir Luke Kernshaw!"

The echo of the name did not come from Julian but from that strange old man who stood rigidly by the door with the draught fluttering his loose garments, and his fierce eyes flashing their light first on one and then on the other. Both of them looked up in surprise at the mention of the name, and again the stranger repeated it in a harsh, strident voice eminently disagreeable.

"Sir Luke Kernshaw!"

"Yes!" said Rebelspear, recovering from his astonishment. "Why do you repeat that name? Do you know Sir Luke?"

"To my cost!"

Rebelspear looked at Julian, and Julian returned his gaze with a significant nod in the direction of the stranger.

" Mad ! "

" No, young gentleman, I am not mad, although I have suffered enough to be so. I could tell you strange things about—but no, at present I will say nothing, the time is not yet come. I have come to see this doctor for my wound ! "

" Your wound ? "

" Behold ! "

This extraordinary creature turned round slowly, and Rebelspear saw on the back of his head a large wound from which flowed the bright scarlet blood down his white locks. His professional instincts at once got the better of his curiosity, and without asking any more questions he attended to the wants of his patient and bound up the cut, which was a very nasty one, while Julian, smoking quietly in his arm-chair, watched the operation in silence. It was a very simple matter, and having bathed the wound, Rebelspear bound a white band of linen round the head of his patient, which, in conjunction with his long white hair and beard, gave him the appearance of one of those venerable prophets who delivered the decrees of Heaven to the Jewish kings. Having lost a good deal of blood, the old man was rather weak, so the young doctor made him take a glass of port wine, and seating him comfortably in a chair, prepared to ask him a few questions, being decidedly puzzled over the whole affair.

" How did you get that cut ? " he asked, going back to his own desk.

" I went forth into the highways and into the byeways to

deliver the message of Heaven, but the daughters of the Gentiles drove over me with the wheels of their chariots, and I was sorely wounded."

"Means he was knocked down by a cab while crossing the street," explained the practical Julian, lighting another cigarette.

The old man turned on him a look full of reproach and reproof.

"You are one of those who dwell in palaces," he said, raising his harsh voice like a trumpet, "one of the many wrapt in loose pleasures to whom the warning is given. I know you, oh, scoffer! for I have beheld you in public places, consorting with the vain ones of this earth."

"And I know you," retorted Julian, with a sneer of contempt. "You are Matthew Malister, that old fanatic, who has been put in jail several times for making rows in the street."

"Malister the Socialist," exclaimed Rebelspear, who was feeling rather bewildered by the biblical phraseology of the old man. "Oh, I know, the Anarchist who addresses meetings in Hyde Park."

"Neither Anarchist nor Socialist," cried Malister with great fervour, "but a Prophet of Doom, who has come from the far East to warn this New Babylon that Heaven is wearied of her vices and of her iniquities."

"A modern John the Baptist," scoffed Julian, looking at the fanatic. "I told you he was mad, Frank. Cracked as the great Bell of Moscow."

"So you say in your blindness, young man," returned Malister, raising his thin hand; "but know that, before the dawn of the new century, this great city will be humbled to the dust. She will call upon her children and they will reply not. She will weep for those that lie dead in the streets and will refuse to be comforted. The song and jest will be silent in her palaces, for the feet of her children go downward to the yawning-grave, and the kings of the earth, the rulers, and princes, will mourn for her desolation."

"Oh! is there going to be a universal war—a battle of Armageddon?" said Rebelspear, with a disbelieving smile. "I've heard such a lot about that sort of thing. The thousand days of Daniel, the opening of the seventh seal, the division of Europe into the ten kingdoms of the ten-horned beast! My good man, all that sort of thing is nonsense; no one believes in such rubbish. I don't wonder you've been locked up, if that's the sort of stuff you talk. Why, science—"

"Science!" interrupted Malister, in a voice of thunder, rising to his feet. "Science can do nothing in the coming trouble. All your learning, all your wealth, all your craft, will avail you nothing when the dead lie unburied in the streets, and London—this mighty city of Nineveh of which you boast—shall be one vast desert. Owls shall build their nests in the dome of St. Paul's—solitude will reign in the palaces of your kings, and—"

"And the New Zealander will sit on the ruins of London Bridge and sketch the ruins of St. Paul's," said Delicker, with scorn. "You are a plagiarist, my good fellow. Macaulay has been before you."

"Fool!" cried the fanatic, fiercely, "your days are numbered; but a short time and the jest on your lips will give place to a cry of terror. Have you not seen the sign which God has set in the heavens to warn this generation of the coming doom ? "

" Oh, the comet ! " observed Rebelspear, quickly, " yes, we have all seen the comet, and a very decent one it is, too ; but what of that ? There have been plenty of comets before now, and plenty of assertions about their striking the earth ; but as up to the present nothing has occurred, I expect we are all safe."

Malister looked at him in a pitying manner, and crossing to him with noiseless swiftness, laid his long hand on the young doctor's shoulder.

" You have helped me in my distress," he said in a softened tone ; " you have poured oil into my wounds and given me wine to drink. Therefore I will be a friend to you, and give you your heart's desire."

" I'm afraid that is beyond your powers," replied the doctor, humouring the old man's weakness ; " I want patients."

" You shall have them in numbers countless as the sands of the sea."

" Oh ! " cried Julian Delicker, rising to his feet, " I'm tired of all this rubbish. If you have finished with this lunatic, Frank, perhaps you'll go and dress."

" Shortly ! shortly ! " replied Rebelspear, struck with the earnestness of the fanatic ; " but first I want to find out something from Mr. Malister."

Julian shrugged his shoulders in a resigned manner, and resumed his seat, while Malister, still standing beside the chair of the young doctor, looked steadily at him with fiery eyes, waiting for him to speak.

" You mentioned the name of Sir Luke Kernshaw," said Rebelspear, after a pause, " and said you knew him to your cost. What did you mean by that ? "

" Mean ! " echoed Malister, fiercely, " I meant that many years ago I had a loving wife who fled with Luke Kernshaw from my home, and left me the wreck I am now."

" A madman," sneered Delicker, cruelly.

" No, sir," retorted Malister, quietly, " not mad. I am as sane as you, fool of fortune that you are. I am only a deceived man, betrayed by a woman, and ruined by a friend, but the way of the evil doer is hard, and after many years I have returned to punish Luke Kernshaw, and demand of him my child."

" Your child ! " cried both young men, in one breath.

" Yes ; my daughter. When my guilty wife fled with her lover, she took with her the child, and though I sought far and wide for them both I never recovered them. But now —now ! the time is at hand."

The same thought flashed across the minds of the young men, as to whether Laura or Eva were the daughter of this strange creature, and Rebelspear, to whom the subject was of most importance, was about to speak, when Malister, whom the thought of his wrongs had worked up into a state of great excitement, burst out into a fierce denunciation of London and its inhabitants.

" Woe ! woe ! woe ! to the evil city—the evil city—the abode of vice and the sink of iniquity. The wrath of Heaven will fall upon it, and none shall live through the days that are to come. I am an outcast, a pariah, a moral leper, yet I have been chosen by the Mighty One to sow the seeds of disease in every street of this iniquitous place. I am the weak that shall confound the strong, and when the shadow of death is over the dome of St. Paul's, then will the inhabitants think upon my warnings of the coming tempest."

"I believe he's talking of a plague," said Delicker, quickly, upon which the fanatic turned on him with a cruel smile.

"You have spoken truly; I am talking of a plague—a plague to which that which desolated mighty London in the evil time of the Stuarts will be as naught. You, man of pleasure, cannot fly from it. You, man of science, cannot defend yourself from it. It will come! it will come and sweep to the tomb all this generation of evil doers. You laugh me to scorn. You say that I am mad—that I lie— that I speak of what cannot be. Doubt me if you like, but believe the sign which God hath set in the heavens as a warning of what is to come."

He tore aside the heavy red curtains that draped the windows, and there, in the darkly blue sky, flashed the mighty comet which had been hanging over Europe for many weeks. Both the young men, educated in the latest sciences of the day, were sceptical of many things, and scoffed at the idea of biblical beliefs, yet, for the moment, they quailed before this new Isaiah with his terrible prophecies of coming doom, the truth of whose mission seemed to be supported by the testimony of the heavens themselves.

Even Delicker, mocker of all things as he was, felt strangely moved for the first time in his idle, egotistical life, but Rebelspear, materialist and man of science, who believed nothing without proof, dismissed the speech of

Malister as the ravings of an over-excited brain, and poured him out another glass of wine.

"Come, come, my good fellow," he said, soothingly, just as if he were petting a fractious child. "You are talking sad nonsense, and if you go on like this they will lock you up as insane. Be advised by me, do not go near Sir Luke Kernshaw, and stop these incoherent ravings, or you will get into trouble. Now that I have done what I can for you, take this glass of wine and go as soon as possible."

"You do not believe my warnings," said Malister, looking sadly at the young doctor. "You think with others that I am mad."

Rebelspear shrugged his shoulders, and smiled meaningly. "My good sir, this is nearly the twentieth century, and I believe nothing without proof. You say a plague is about to devastate London. I say such a thing cannot occur—at least, it is highly improbable. In the middle ages, when London was badly drained, and the inhabitants badly housed, paying no attention to the laws of health, such a thing was likely, and, of course, took place; but now, when everything has been done for the public health that science can do, I'm afraid the plague you prophesy will never come off. As to the comet, we have explained away all these things."

"Have you explained away God?"

"I don't want to enter into a theological discussion," said Rebelspear, rather nettled. "I have done what I can for you; so please withdraw."

Julian nodded approvingly, but Malister still stood quietly by the window in an attitude of utter dejection.

"I have warned you to fly, and you will not fly; so when

the Burning Sickness comes upon you, then you will be lost like all other dwellers in this city. Yet, young man, I see you have a kind heart to assist the weak and suffering, so I will save you in spite of yourself. Gold I have none to repay your aid, but I will give you a more valuable reward. I will bestow on you life, and when all around you are falling under the scourge of God, you will walk unharmed through the terrors that surround you."

"Mere ravings," muttered Julian with a yawn.

"I will tell you both my story," said Malister, without taking any notice of the interruption, "and you can judge for yourself as to whether I speak truth or not."

Julian made a gesture of impatience, but Rebelspear hesitated. He was greatly puzzled by the quiet demeanour of one whom he could not but regard as a madman, and was anxious to hear the justification he proposed to make of his eccentric conduct. For some time past, this man had been a prominent figure in London police courts, owing to the crowds he attracted in the streets, while preaching his terrible warning of the coming plague, and Rebelspear, now that the fanatic was willing to confide in him, felt very desirous to discover if there was any method in his madness.

"You can go, Julian," he said at last, making up his mind. "I will follow you later on, but meanwhile I want to hear what Mr. Malister has to say for himself."

"It's only half-past ten," said Julian, looking at his watch, and comparing it with the clock, "and if we arrive at Kernshaw's at twelve, it will be time enough, so I also will wait and hear this story."

" You can if you like," observed Malister, slowly, " but you will not believe what I say."

" Very probably not ; but I'm fond of romance, and your ' Thousand and Second Night ' will no doubt be amusing."

The fanatic cast a look of profound contempt on this frivolous speaker, and still standing by the window with the pale phosphorescent gleam of the comet visible behind him, told his story to those two young men, who both listened with great attention to his strange narrative, but with widely different feelings, the contempt Julian evinced for this latter-day prophet not being shared by Dr. Rebelspear.

The warning which had been given to thousands, and which had many times cost Malister his liberty, was now being given to them, but believe, or disbelieve, as they would, neither of them, occupied as they were, could help being fascinated by the *bizarre* story told so dramatically by one who called himself the Prophet of Doom.

CHAPTER III.

"What is man but a vain shadow, that vanisheth when the sun of prosperity ceaseth to shine." In me, O my friends, you behold an illustration of this saying! I am now old and frail, but I was once as young and comely as you are. In the days of my youth I rejoiced greatly, doing that which seemed good in mine eyes, nor dreamed that my life would be otherwise than pleasant and prosperous. Wealth, health, and friends were mine, and I took unto myself a fair wife, whom I cherished tenderly; therefore in the pride of my heart I laughed to scorn the thought of trouble, but God in His mysterious wisdom chose me as His messenger, to declare His commands to this generation of evil-doers, and led me through many trials to the understanding of the mission He desired me to fulfil. Up to the age of forty years my life was gay and ca.eless, with no thought of the morrow, or regret for the past; but when the appointed time came, I was bereft of all I held most dear, and exiled by the fiat of Heaven to distant lands. I there prepared myself in solitude for the part I had to play in this last drama of the nineteenth century.

This Luke Kernshaw of whom you speak was my trusted friend, and being an old schoolfellow we had been bound by the closest ties of amity for many years. My wife was fair, and we had one child, a little daughter, who was the delight of my heart; so, with all these joys I was perfectly happy. Friend, wife, and child, what more could I desire from Heaven? but, alas! in my enjoyment of the blessings of God I forgot the Giver, nor thanked Him for His fatherly care, therefore was I bitterly punished. Like Job I was blessed above all my fellow-creatures, and like Job I was in a single day abased to the dust by misfortune. "The heart knoweth its own bitterness," saith the preacher, and well did I understand the saying when I found myself deprived of friend, wife, and child by the justice of Heaven.

In those days I travelled a great deal and often went about alone, as my wife was delicate, and did not care about moving from her quiet home. During my frequent absence, Kernshaw was a constant visitor to my house, and, blind fool that I was, I encouraged his visits, never for a moment dreaming of the base purpose which underlay his professions of ardent friendship. At last the blow fell—fell when I least expected it, and I returned from the north of Scotland to find that my treacherous friend and guilty wife had fled to the Continent, taking with them my only child. Filled with wrath and the fierce indignation of a wronged man, I pursued them at once, but so successfully had they arranged their flight that I was unable to discover their hiding-place. Misfortune never comes singly, however, and after experiencing the full bitterness of this terrible calamity another blow fell. Owing to various causes connected with commercial depression and the stoppage of a bank, I lost all my fortune, and thus found myself deprived of all that made life worth living.

All these misfortunes told so severely on my health that I became seriously ill with brain fever, and for many weeks lay sick unto death in an out-of-the-way village in France. I wanted to die, for I had nothing left me for which to desire life, but God in His inscrutable mercy preserved my life and my reason, and from that bed of sickness I arose to move onward in the appointed path, the end of which I am now nearing.

On recovering my health I learned that my guilty wife had died of an attack of typhoid fever, and also that a distant relative had died and left me a large sum of money. I at once went in search of my former friend and my child, but was unable to find traces of either, so in despair I abandoned the hope of punishing the one or recovering the other. The world was now hateful to me, owing to my misfortunes, so, inspired by Heaven, I departed to the East in search of peace, if not happiness, and it was there, amid the melancholy deserts of Arabia, that God revealed to me my destiny and sent me forth to this evil world as a Prophet of Doom to foretell the calamities which are now about to fall upon the generation who have forgotten Him.

After staying some time in Alexandria I went on to Cairo and remained many weeks in that ancient city of the Mamelukes, passing every day in the most agreeable manner in visiting the Pyramids, the antiquities of the city, the mosques, and various other objects of interest. I also went up the Nile and saw those splendid ruins of old Egypt which rise amid the desert sands under the hot glow of the

Eastern sun. While sleeping in one of these Pharaohonic temples, I had a dream which I had no doubt came from Heaven, for in it I was bidden to go to the South and there search for the means by which God intended to punish the luxury and evil living of these days.

Acting under an uncontrollable impulse, I took ship at Alexandria and sailed down the Red Sea to the port of Jiddah, intending from thence to go to Mecca, the Holy City of the Turkish world. Having a considerable amount of money at my command, I hired many camels and attendants, and, in spite of the warnings of the British Consul at Jiddah, began my journey to the tomb of Mahomet. For many days we journeyed through the dreary wastes of sand which environ the Holy City, and at last, through the treachery or mistake of the guide, we lost our way. Looking upon this as a judgment on them for taking an infidel to the tomb of their prophet, my attendants would have killed me, but being mounted on a swift dromedary I was fortunate enough to escape, and fled for many hours from these bloodthirsty fanatics. In spite, however, of my swift dromedary, I should doubtless have been overtaken, when Heaven interposed, and all my pursuers were overwhelmed in a simoon. In company with all the rest I had flung myself on the ground until the terror of this sandstorm was passed, but when I arose to my feet I saw no trace of men or camels, all being buried beneath mountains of yellow sand. Even my dromedary had shared the same fate; so here was I in the lonely desert without a guide, a camel, a drop of water, or a morsel of bread; with nothing but my life and the protection of God.

At first I gave way to despair; for, desire death as much as possible, it is nevertheless terrible to find oneself in such a position, but some inward voice advised me to be of good cheer, and I set forward to cross the desert in the hope of discovering some Bedouin encampment, and thus preserving my life. Of my sufferings I need not tell you, but you can guess how terrible they were in my then state of destitution; and the sun rose, the sun set, the day dawned, the night fell with still that illimitable waste of sand around me, and the burning sun overhead.

Towards the close of the second day I could no longer proceed, being weak with hunger and parched with thirst, so I lay down on the hot sand to die just at the hour of sunset. Suddenly, in front of the blood-red disc, which was sinking behind the level edge of the desert, I saw the silhouette of a vast city. Towers, domes, minarets, walls all loomed blackly against the crimson sky, and in spite of my fancy that it was a mirage or a spectral illusion created by my want of food, it certainly looked substantial enough. The sight put new strength into me, as I thought I was now saved; so with great difficulty I managed to struggle on until I arrived under the frowning walls which protected this city of the desert from the encroaching sands. The enormous gates which were set in a horse-shoe archway were wide open, and by these I sank down, calling hoarsely for help. No one replied, and although I cried again and again in a weak voice, I heard no answering cry, so I came to the conclusion that the city was deserted. Suddenly I heard the sound of running water, and dragging myself along to the musical gurgle, I found a clear stream of water spouting from the wall into a shallow trough. Oh! the ecstasy of that long draught of cold clear water—after all my torments it was like the gift of a new life.

Thus refreshed, I went slowly along the narrow streets to see whether I could meet with a human being; for the horror of this silent city struck me with a sense of terror. The moon was now shining palely in the dark sky, and under her silver beams I saw that the massive buildings on each side were purely Oriental in their architecture, with closely latticed windows bulging from their ornate fronts, and massively barred doors set in trefoil arches. All at once I shrieked with terror; for, on emerging into a large square, I stumbled over the corpse of a man: then I saw another and another, and as I took in the whole scene, beheld this immense space covered with the dead bodies of men like some terrible battle-field. On recovering from my first terror, I examined the bodies, but could see no signs of blood or wounds, only a frozen look of abject dread stamped upon each face. The spectacle of this graveyard was awe-inspiring in the extreme, and I could not guess the reason of this sudden mortality among the inhabitants of this lonely city. No sound except the musical splashing of fountains, no light save the serene splendour of the moon, and amid the stately palaces, which environed the square, nothing but this army of the dead, suddenly stricken by the hand of God by some terrible plague.

As I stood there frozen with terror, and wondering what I was to do, and whether I was under the influence of some frightful nightmare, I heard the sound of a human voice, loud and shrill, raised in a measured chant. Nearer and

B

nearer it came, until at length I saw a tall man in a floating, white robe, step across the innumerable dead bodies and come straight to where I was standing. He was an old, old man, something like what I am now in appearance, and with uplifted hands he recited some melancholy verses from the Koran in sonorous Arabic.

When he beheld me he stopped; and, seeing from my dress that I was an European, addressed me in French. As he did so, I laughed aloud, so grotesque seemed the contrast of the gay Gallic tongue with the terrible mysticism of the place where we were standing.

"Giaour, why dost thou laugh?" said the old man in tones of reproof; "rather weep at the sight of this desolation amid which thou findest thyself."

"I laughed because you spoke French," I replied, after a pause. "This is like a city of the Thousand and One Nights, and to hear the French tongue in this hideous solitude seems ludicrous in the extreme."

"I have been to the Mother of Cities, even Stamboul, O Giaour, and there I learned the wisdom of the Franks. But tell me, O wanderer, wherefore art thou here in this city accursed of Allah?"

Upon being asked this question, I told the old dervish all my trials and adventures, upon which, after some thought, he motioned to me to follow him, and leading me to a house on one side of the square, set wine and food before me. While I was eating he said nothing, but eyed me keenly, and when I had finished, he flung open the leaves of a copy of the Koran, which stood near him on a reading desk, and read the first verse upon which his eye alighted. It seemed to satisfy him, for he seated himself beside me and told me the reason of the strange sights I had seen in this city of the dead.

"Wonderful are the ways of Allah, O Giaour," he said, solemnly stroking his beard ; "for know that I behold in you a messenger of doom to the infidel, as I have been to the faithful. The All-Merciful hath chosen thee to receive from my lips the warning which thou shalt deliver to the children of Gehenna, who dwell in the West, and, should they laugh thy words to scorn, upon them will fall the same doom which hath descended upon these people of this proud city."

After this strange exordium, the meaning of which I could not understand, he proceeded with his tale.

"Know, O Giaour, that this is the famous city of Naı which has been shut out by the desert sands for all time from the prying eyes of the restless West. The people who dwelt herein were proud and haughty, and although they received the faith of the one true God from the mouth of Mahomet himself, yet did they fall away in the lust of their hearts. I was one of the children of this city, and having become a Dervish, wandered away from my birthplace to the Mother of Cities, where dwells the Padishaw. There I consumed my days and nights in learning, and I saw the exceeding wickedness of men. Then, moved by Allah, I returned to this city and called upon my fellow-townsmen to return to their former simple ways lest the doom of Allah should fall upon them. They laughed me to scorn and mocked my words, therefore I fulfilled my mission.

"This bottle," continued the dervish, drawing a phial

from the folds of his robe, "contains the germs of a deadly plague called the Burning Sickness, and if sprinkled in the street will spread through the whole city, slaying all and sparing none. Where I obtained it I need not tell thee; but fulfilling the will of Allah, I broke one of these phials in yonder square, and so the plague swept through the city of Nar, sparing none. Man, woman, and child, all perished as thou seest, and I alone am left alive to tell thee the tale, O, Heaven-guided one! and to deliver to thee this phial, so that thou mayest fulfil the will of Allah in the West."

I was much astonished at this strange recital, and demanded of the dervish what I was to do, and how I was to return to civilisation.

"Go!" he said, giving me the phial, "and at the western gate thou wilt find a camel and a guide who will lead thee back to Jiddah, whence thou can'st return to thine own land. When there, call upon thy fellowmen to repent, and if they scorn thee, break that phial in the street of the most populous city. Then will Azrael draw his sword, nor sheath it until all are destroyed."

After saying these words he bade me sleep, which I did soundly, being worn out with fatigue; but at early dawn the dervish woke me, and leading me himself to the western gate, placed me on the camel; then bidding me good-bye, went back into the city. Just outside the gate I found the guide mounted on another camel, and this man, who spoke no word during the journey, guided me to Jiddah. On arriving at the port my guide disappeared, and I sailed by the first ship to Alexandria. Unfortunately, however, I was wrecked by a storm and was detained for many years a prisoner by the Bedouins, but at last I managed to escape and came straight to London to preach the Word of the Lord. I have been placed in prison, I have been scorned, I have been maltreated, but I still lift up my voice to call this mighty city to repentance. They will not hearken to my words, the appointed time is at hand, and within three days will the Burning Sickness rage among them until none will be left alive, like the citizens of that Arabian Nar.

CHAPTER IV.

THE FANTASY OF A MADMAN'S BRAIN.

THIS strange narrative having thus come to an end, there was silence in the room for a few minutes, each of the three men present being occupied with his own thoughts. Malister was dreaming of his past troubles and his terrible mission, but the same idea was in the minds of Rebelspear and his friend. The old man was mad, quite mad, for surely such a *bizarre* tale could have emanated from nowhere but the fantastic brain of an insane person. It was a reminiscence of the "Arabian Nights," filled with the grim superstitions of the East, and that an educated man, for so Malister appeared to be, should tell such a tissue of grotesque horrors as his actual experience, proved that his brain was not properly balanced. Such a monstrous story might have been believed in the days of Mediævalism, when the world was supposed to be full of such unknown horrors; but to give these fantasies an actual existence at the end of the nineteenth century was too absurd, and both the young doctor and Julian felt it to be so. The latter was the first to break the silence which followed the narration of this Thousand and Second Night, and burst out into a hearty laugh.

3²

" I like fairy stories," he said, mockingly, " and yours is one of the best I have heard."

" You don't believe me, sir ? "

" Hardly. I've travelled myself and know the romances of voyagers. I suspect you have met Sultana Scheherazade, my friend, and she has related to you a story."

" You are like the inhabitants of the city of Nar," said the fanatic, sternly. " You mock at my words and look upon my warning as a capital jest, but beware, the time is at hand, and before the end of the present week you will fall a victim to the Burning Sickness."

" Well, I was wishing for a plague, Frank," observed Julian, turning to his friend ; " and now it is likely that we are going to have one. Pooh ! who ever heard such rubbish. A plague in London ! A fairy tale from the deserts of Arabia ! A bogey to frighten women. My good Mr. Malister, Socialist and Romancer, you had better go at once to Colney Hatch."

" Scoff on, oh, man of pleasure ! " said Malister, taking up his hat. " Another week will prove the truth of my words, and when you die in the streets by the Burning Sickness, you will remember my warning."

Julian shrugged his shoulders with infinite contempt and turned away, but Dr. Rebelspear, who had hitherto kept silence, now suddenly addressed himself to the old man.

" I am a man of science," he said, slowly, " and I believe nothing without proof. You say this dervish gave you a phial containing the plague you speak of. May I see that phial ? "

" Behold ! nor doubt the truth of my words."

He drew a slender bottle of cut crystal from his pocket and presented it to Rebelspear, who received it with lively curiosity. The phial was about as long and thick as the middle finger of a man's hand, and contained some jet black fluid which looked like ink. There was no stopper, as the glass was perfect at both ends, and the only way to get at the contents would be by breaking it, as the dervish described. Rebelspear held it in his right hand under the bright glare of the electric light, and the crystal cut in many facets flashed and glittered like diamonds, which intensified the sombre look of the thin, black line, within which, according to Malister, was the deadly liquid containing the germs of the plague.

"So with this little bottle you purpose to depopulate London," said Rebelspear, disbelievingly balancing it in his hand.

"You, as a doctor, should know how germs multiply," replied Malister quietly. "I break that in the street and the infusoria within will come in contact with the outer air. When that takes place there is no hope for this evil city; for every atom will increase a thousand-fold, and the wind will bear the seeds of death into every street, into every house, into every room. The air will be heavy with the breath of the plague—the strong man shall fall prone in the midst of his toil—the orgy of the voluptuary will end in death—no more shall be heard the sounds of labour or pleasure, and grass will grow in the populous streets of this great city. The living will have no time to bury the dead, and they will lie at the doors of their palaces with no one to heed them. Woe! woe! to this mighty city which hath wearied Heaven by her crimes, for the end is at hand and the pride of the earth will be humbled to the dust."

Rebelspear listened to this biblical address with an unmoved countenance, and handed back the phial to Malister, who replaced it in his pocket.

"I don't believe that bottle contains all the woes you have described," he said, coolly; "but let us grant, for the sake of argument, that it does. If so, do you think it a wise or a pious thing to sow the seeds of a terrible disease in the midst of your fellow-countrymen?"

"They will not listen to my voice," cried Malister, with fervid fierceness. "I have called to the sheep but they will not obey the voice of the shepherd. All the vices of the earth are to be found in this wealthy city of palaces. They are drunken with their wealth, and filled with pride, when thinking of their strength. Three months have I preached in the public places, and ever I have been railed and scoffed at. Now, the measure of their iniquities is full and runneth over, for the Most High is wearied of their sin and perverseness. Three more days will I call upon them to repent, and if they do not I must obey the words of Heaven, and bring upon this generation of mockers the doom which they have called upon themselves."

"By the way," said Julian, suddenly interrupting this long address, "if this plague kills everyone, how did your dervish and guide escape?"

Malister drew forth from another pocket a phial similar to the first, but it contained no black liquid, and, in fact, looked as if it contained nothing at all; and, moreover, instead of being sealed at both ends, it had a glass stopper, which could easily be unscrewed when the contents were required to be made use of.

"This is a cure for the Burning Sickness," he said, giving the phial to Rebelspear ; "it contains a liquid clear as crystal. Three drops in a tumbler of water will change it to a liquid the colour of blood. Whomsoever drinks it will be cured at once. The dervish and my guide were both seized by the plague, but were cured as I have told you, and the phial was given to me so as to preserve me through the horrors that are to come."

Rebelspear was as incredulous over this second phial as he was over the first, and gave it back to Malister with a contemptuous smile, but, to his surprise, the old man refused to receive it.

"No !" he said, waving his thin hand ; "you have been kind to me, and I promised to aid you. No patients have you now, but in a week you will have many. The contents of that phial will cure them, and every drop is worth its weight in gold. Take it, sir, and when you find my words come true forget not that a kind action ever brings its reward."

"But what about yourself, Mr. Malister ? If this plague does come you will fall a victim to it."

"I care not," replied the fanatic, gloomily ; "I have nothing left to live for. When I break this phial in the streets and sow the germs of the plague my mission will be ended."

"But your daughter ?"

"Ah, my daughter! True ; I had forgotten her, but perchance she is dead. I will seek out Sir Luke Kernshaw and demand of him my child."

" Sir Luke has two daughters," said Julian, quickly.

"Is that so? Then he will lose both. He will suffer the agonies he inflicted upon me. His children will die of the Burning Sickness, and he himself will go down to the grave, but not before I come face to face with him once more."

" His daughters shall not die if this antidote is any good," said Rebelspear, bluntly, putting the phial in his desk, " for I am in love with one of them."

" She will bring you woe, oh, foolish man ! As the father is so shall be the child, and if you wed with a daughter of that wicked man you will be punished. But there ! there ! marry if you will, for in a few weeks you will all be dead in the streets of your city."

" If you think Sir Luke Kernshaw has treated you badly, why don't you go and see him at once ?" asked the young doctor with a yawn.

" No !" cried Malister, putting on his hat; " I will not see him ! I will not speak to him until the doom falls upon him and his. When his two fair daughters lie dead at his feet ; when he himself stands on the threshold of the grave, then will I appear and show him this marred visage, this bent form, to recall to him the man he so deeply wronged. And now, doctor, I will take my leave. You have poured oil into my wounds, you have given me wine to drink, and in the time of coming trouble you will find that my grati- tude will save you from death. For three days will I call aloud in the public streets and summon all to repentance. If none reply or hearken to my voice, then will this great city, the pride of the earth, be levelled to the dust. Spiders will weave their webs in her palaces, and the nations will weep far off with great wailing at her fall."

He had thrown open the door during this speech, and the inrushing draught fluttered his loose garments as he faded out of the room like some unhappy ghost. Even after he had vanished the two young men could hear his harsh voice raised in fierce denunciations, and then they heard the front door close sharply as he went out into the silent night on his mission of doom.

"Oh, dear, dear!" yawned Julian, stretching himself, "who ever heard such a lot of rubbish? Why don't they shut up that old lunatic? If he goes about like this he'll frighten all the old women into fits."

"I don't believe his Arabian story, certainly," said Rebelspear, slowly, "but he might have some germs in that bottle likely to cause trouble. I almost wish I had taken it off him."

"Nonsense, my dear Frank. The man's as mad as a hatter, and has infected you with his insanity. A plague, indeed! who ever heard of such rubbish?"

"Well, if the plague does come, I've got the cure!"

"No doubt, the cure and the germs are much about a muchness. If this Burning Sickness does turn up I'll come to you to be cured, Frank; but I can't congratulate you on your first patient."

"Oh, something is better than nothing."

"No doubt, and as you have at last really made a start, just jump into your evening dress and come to Kernshaw's at once to tell Eva Kcrushaw about your first success."

"If I told her all it would rather frighten her," said Rebelspear, with a laugh, as he left the room.

"Very likely it would," muttered Delicker, when he was left alone, "that old madman's story was as weird as any of Poe's fancies. I don't care about such horrors. I don't believe his 'Arabian Nights,' but that story about Kernshaw might be true, and it is that which has sent him mad. Perhaps one of those two girls is his daughter. Humph! I shouldn't wonder. They're not a bit alike."

He put the question to Rebelspear when they were driving along in a hansom towards Park Lane, and the young doctor agreed that such a thing might not be impossible.

"At all events," he said, after a pause, "Kernshaw was not married when he went off with Malister's wife, so the old man's child will be the elder of the two."

"And which is the elder—Eva or Laura?"

"I don't know," replied Rebelspear, rather puzzled, "but now I have the curiosity to find out."

"If it's Eva!" said Julian, laughing, "you can marry her, and she'll bring you her father's plague and many patients as her dowry."

"And suppose it is Laura?"

"Oh, she's a plague in herself," was the quick rejoinder, "a perfect vixen that girl, whom I should not like to offend. I think she is very beautiful, but I doubt her temper. No, no, my boy, whichever of the two is Malister's daughter you marry Eva—that is if Laura will let you."

"Let me! why, how can she stop me?"

"I don't know, but she'll try, my dear Frank. If this

Burning Sickness does come and kill off Laura Kernshaw, it will be a good thing for you."

"And why?"

"Because she's Lady Macbeth and Messalina rolled into one."

CHAPTER V.

DAY AND NIGHT.

Sir Luke Kernshaw was not a particularly wicked man, and his sins proceeded rather from the curse of idleness than from a bad disposition. Never was the adage that "Satan finds some mischief still for idle hands to do," better exemplified than in his case, as, having had plenty of money all his life, and no occupation, he amused himself by obeying every trivial impulse of his mind. He gambled in a moderate fashion, and did not lay himself out to be of service to his fellow-men; but although he had no very exalted idea of female virtue, until he eloped with the wife of his dearest friend, he had not been guilty of any social crime, and passed among his set as a very decent sort of fellow.

When Malister was married, Kernshaw had acted as best man to the groom, and even then had been struck with the charms of the bride. Wishing, however, to remain faithful to his old schoolfellow, he had assiduously kept away from the house, but having been persuaded by Malister to stay with him for a time in the country, he had yielded without further struggle to what he regarded as his fate. The end came in due course, and the guilty pair fled to the

Continent, but not for long did they enjoy their unhallowed felicity, for while waiting for the divorce they thought Malister would obtain, the unhappy woman died of typhoid fever, and Kernshaw was left alone with her child. True, however, to the memory of the woman whom he had ruined, he looked after the little girl, and when he returned to England a year later, she was regarded by the friends of the baronet as his own child. This idea Kernshaw did not deny, and when he married and a daughter was born to him, both children were brought up as his offspring with the utmost impartiality.

Malister had of course disappeared to the East, where he remained among the Bedouins for twenty years, and during this interval Lady Kernshaw died, leaving her daughter to be reared with the child of the woman whom her husband had loved and ruined. Now that the unhappy Malister, frenzied by the recollection of his wrongs, and armed with a terrible means of revenge, had returned to London, Sir Luke Kernshaw was living at his house in Park Lane with his two daughters, Laura and Eva, both of whom were much admired in London society.

Laura was tall, dark, and majestic, with the imperious mien of a queen, and a fiery disposition kept well under control by her strong nature; while Eva was a slender, delicate girl, with golden hair, and a somewhat shrinking manner, who differed in every way from her Cleopatra-like sister. A celebrated painter had taken them as models for a picture, which he called "Day and Night," which fancy taking the ear of society, the two sisters were known to everyone by these titles, and certainly Laura represented dark-browed Night as admirably as her timid, golden-haired sister did Day.

Sir Luke was very fond of them both, and as the old scandal of his youth had long since died away, no one for a moment dreamed that one of the sisters so-called was not his child, and so like were they in many respects that they were generally taken for twins. Who was the elder no person ever discovered, and the girls finding that such a thing piqued the curiosity of their friends, always laughingly declined to tell their ages, although they themselves did not know there was any reason that they should keep them secret. Kernshaw, however, was not ill-pleased at this innocent mystification, as he was so fond of the child of his old mistress that he did not want her taken away from him, and he dreaded lest Malister should return to London again and claim his daughter.

Twenty years, however, had passed away without such a claim being made, and Sir Luke was quite satisfied that the old folly was dead and forgotten, when he was startled to see the name of Matthew Malister appear frequently in the papers as a disturber of the public peace. At once he remembered his old schoolfellow, and obtaining a glimpse of this new prophet, when he was holding a meeting in Hyde Park, he recognised the man he had wronged, in spite of the change in his appearance affected by the lapse of years. Every day he expected to see Malister appear and claim his child, but day after day passed and there was no appearance of his former friend, so Kernshaw again breathed freely, as seeing that the papers declared the fanatic to be a madman, he thought that he had forgotten all about his

2 B

lost child. Still, to make things more secure, he determined to take his daughters to the Continent until Malister should disappear, or be shut up in some asylum as a madman, and this ball to which Dr. Rebelspear and Delicker were coming, was given as a farewell to London society by the hospitable baronet.

It was twelve o'clock when the young men arrived at the house in Park Lane, and the ball was in full swing. The large dancing-room was lined with people, and over the polished floor glided the dancers to the sensuous strains of the last new valse, "Il y'etait un fois." Many coloured flowers decorated the walls, and under the steady gleam of the electric light moved the brilliant throng of guests, laughing and jesting as their feet moved in rhythmical measure to the steady beat of the music. Remembering what the old man had said, Rebelspear, standing at the door of the room under an arch of flowers, thought that the scene looked like some weird dance of death, in which grisly skeletons, invisible to the eye, mingled with the giddy crowd. The glare of the light, the heavy perfumes of the flowers, the swaying forms of the dancers, all intoxicated him as with the fumes of opium smoke, and he almost expected to see letters of fire flash out from the flower-wreathed walls, warning the heedless throng of the coming doom, as happened in old time at the feast of Belshazzar.

Sir Luke, with whom the young man was not a favourite, received him as coldly as hospitality would permit, but Julian Delicker, the wealthy young man, received a much warmer welcome, and turning away with a conventionally smiling face to hide his aching heart, Rebelspear could not help comparing the difference of their receptions.

"Money can do anything," he muttered, bitterly, pushing his way through the crowd in search of Eva; "it can even make that old baronet kindly."

Eva was standing in the centre of half-a-dozen gentlemen, who were talking to her about the last frivolous event of the day, but when she saw Rebelspear she flushed quickly with pleasure.

"Good-evening," she said, with well-bred composure, conscious that the eyes of the world were on them. "Have you been here long?"

"I have only just arrived, but I trust I am not too late for a dance?"

Eva pursed up her rosy lips, and looked at her programme with a roguish laugh.

"I'm afraid you are, Dr. Rebelspear. My programme is filled up twice over."

"That is the penalty of beauty, Miss Kernshaw," said one of the gentlemen, politely.

"A very pleasant penalty, at all events," returned the girl, laughing. "Well, Dr. Rebelspear, you may look at my programme while I am engaged in dancing," and giving her card to Rebelspear she moved off with a gay nod on the arm of the gentleman who had paid her the compliment.

Frank looked at the programme without delay, and saw with delight that his initials were placed against several dances by the hand of Eva herself; so being thus certain of a pleasant evening, he lounged contentedly against the wall until Miss Kernshaw returned.

"Ah, here is Dr. Rebelspear!"

"And in a brown study."

These two remarks came from Julian Delicker, and from a lady, who was leaning on his arm. A handsome woman she was, with boldly cut features, masses of dark hair, and an imperious mien which admirably suited her regal beauty. This was Night, the sister of Eva, and it was easy to see that she was in love with the young doctor, for every flash of her dark eyes betrayed the secret of her heart. Those eyes, that could look cruelly enough at times, were now bent upon Frank with a languid, melting gaze that made him flush with annoyance as he saw the significant smile on the face of his friend.

"How do you do, Miss Kernshaw?" he said, quickly. "I am just waiting for your sister, who has promised me the next dance. I hope I am to have the same favour from yourself."

"I am sorry, Dr. Rebelspear, but I am engaged," replied Laura, coldly, with a flash of jealousy in her eyes, and walked quickly away with Julian.

Rebelspear stood fixed with astonishment at this singular conduct, not knowing what he had done to deserve such severe treatment. He was a clever fellow in many respects, this young doctor, but he was remarkably stupid with regard to the fair sex; otherwise he would certainly have known at once that Laura Kernshaw's refusal was dictated by jealousy. Not being versed in feminine subtility, however, he was puzzling on the matter when he heard the voice of Eva, and on turning round, beheld her by his side, waiting for him to give her his arm.

"I don't want to dance at present," she said, quickly, slipping her hand within his arm. "Come to the conservatory; I have something to ask you."

Rebelspear was only too delighted to thus have a chance of a quiet talk, and they soon found a secluded nook behind a screen of ferns, where they could see without being seen.

"O, Frank," began Eva, hurriedly, "papa is so angry with me—so terribly angry!"

"And I am the cause, I suppose?"

"Yes, partly. I was looking at the ring you gave me, and Laura saw me doing so. She asked me whose it was, and, very foolishly, I mentioned your name, upon which she went to papa and told him all sorts of dreadful things."

"But why should your sister be my enemy? I have never harmed her."

"She is not your enemy, Frank, but she is mine, because you love me."

"Really?" said the young doctor, rather embarrassed. "I'm afraid you are making a mistake, Eva. Laura is one of the belles of the season, and can look higher than a poor doctor like me. Besides, I love no one but you."

"Yes, I know that, and so does papa. He wants me to give you up; but I'll never do it, Frank! I will wait till you are earning a good income, and then we will marry."

"I hope that day is not far off," said Rebelspear, cheerfully; "at all events, I have made a good start. I had my first patient to-night."

"O, Frank!"

"He was not a very opulent patient. Still he was better

than nothing, my dear.　Besides, he told me all kinds of strange things."

" What about ? "

" Oh, I cannot tell you now ; but, Eva! " exclaimed Frank, recollecting what Malister had told him about his child, " tell me which is the elder of you two girls ? "

" I cannot, Frank, because I don't know ! "

" My dear Eva, that is absurd, you must know."

" If I did, I would tell you, Frank ; but—really I think we are the same age."

" Twins ? "

" No—not twins."

" Well, if you are not twins, one of you must be older than the other."

" All I know is this, Frank, that Laura was brought up away from home until I was five years of age.　Then papa brought her to me, and while making friends as children do, I said I was five.　She also said she was five, so you see I know nothing at all."

" Do you think she is older than you ? "

" I don't know ! We have always passed for being the same age—in fact, twins, but we are not."

The young doctor felt rather perplexed at all this mystery, which had no doubt been arranged by Sir Luke to guard against any claim made by Malister for his child. One of these girls was the elder, but both were ignorant of their real age, so if Malister had appeared it would have been impossible for him to claim his child.　Sir Luke was the only person who knew which was which, and he certainly would keep silence on the subject.　Rebelspear, however, having learned so curiously a portion of Sir Luke's past history, determined to use his knowledge to further his chances of marrying Eva, and made up his mind to call upon the baronet the next day.

"I really don't think your father is acting fairly, Eva," he said, after a pause. "I am young, and likely to succeed in my profession. We love one another dearly, so I will call and ask him to sanction our engagement."

"He'll never do that, Frank. Even if he wanted to, Laura would not let him."

Frank felt inclined to use a very bad word in connection with this interfering Laura, but suppressing the inclination, he took Eva in his arms and kissed her fondly.

"Hope for the best, my dearest. I will see your father to-morrow, and I have every hope of gaining his consent to our marriage. I wish, however, I could find out which of you two girls is the elder."

"Why, Frank?"

"Because I think such knowledge would remove every obstacle to our marriage."

CHAPTER VI.

THE next day Frank Rebelspear carried out his determination to see Sir Luke Kernshaw, and took his way towards Park Lane about the hour of three o'clock. It was no use waiting for patients, as after that famous first one, no other person had come for medical aid; but Frank was not thinking of his practice so much as of the attitude he intended to take towards Sir Luke. Chance, in the person of Malister, had placed in his hands a weapon which, if used dexterously, might force the baronet to consent to the wished-for engagement; nor did Frank think he was acting wrongly in taking advantage of such a chance.

The revelations of the old fanatic had startled Rebelspear and considerably altered his opinion regarding Sir Luke, whom he had hitherto regarded as the soul of honour. Now, however, that the mask was torn off and the baronet appeared as a false friend who had ruined a woman, and a man who was wrongfully withholding a dearly loved child from her father, Rebelspear felt that it was only just that he should be met with his own weapons. This seemingly honest man was guilty of the most ignoble conduct, and sooner than let it be known to the world, he would certainly give his daughter—supposing Eva to be his daughter —to the impecunious young doctor. Frank had no intention of using threats to gain his ends; all he intended to do was to tell Sir Luke what he knew, and then await the result of such a revelation. If Sir Luke would let him marry Eva and help him in his profession, all would go well; but if not, poor Rebelspear did not see what was to be done. True, he might invoke the aid of Malister to take away his child, but then no one but Sir Luke knew which was the child in question; and even if he did tell, it might turn out that Laura was Malister's daughter, in which case Rebelspear would gain no benefit.

As to the old madman's weird story of the coming plague, Rebelspear dismissed that at once from his mind, and never even looked at the antidote, after he had placed it away in his desk. All he desired was to marry Eva, and when once that wish was gratified, plague or no plague, it mattered nothing to him. If the plague did not come—and he never for a moment fancied it would—things would go on just the same; but if the city did fall under the curse of the Burning Sickness he would, by using the cure given to him by the old prophet, be able to save both himself and Eva from the terrible visitation.

Sir Luke Kernshaw was in his study when Rebelspear arrived, and when the young doctor entered the room he was received somewhat stiffly by the occupant. The baronet knew quite well what was the object of Frank's visit, but feigned ignorance, so as to make the interview as embarrassing as possible. Notwithstanding his disapproval of Rebelspear, however, he could not help acknowledging

to himself that this impecunious suitor was a wonderfully
well-looking youth, and in his innermost heart could hardly
blame his daughter for the partiality she displayed towards
this medical Adonis.   Still, good looks did not, in the
baronet's opinion, compensate for a lack of income, and, like
Pharaoh of old, he hardened his heart towards the comeliness
of the unlucky suitor.

. The baronet was a well-preserved old gentleman, ex-
quisitely dressed in a somewhat old-fashioned style, and
bore himself in a stiff, dignified manner, which formed a
marked contrast to the free and easy demeanour of the
later generation.

"You wish to see me, I believe, Dr. Rebelspear?" he
said, courteously, when his visitor was seated.

"Yes, sir, on very particular business."

"Indeed !   Connected with your profession, I presume?"

"No, Sir Luke, connected with my happiness."

Kernshaw raised his eyebrows a little, and slowly tapped
the table before him with his gold-rimmed *pince-nez.*

"I'm afraid I can do nothing in that way.   I certainly
might be able to help you in your profession, but as to
happiness, my dear sir, no mortal can bestow that gift."

"It is in your power to be more than mortal then," said
Frank, impulsively, "for you can make me very, very
happy."

"And how, Dr. Rebelspear?"

"By allowing me to marry your daughter, Eva."

Forewarned is forearmed ; and Sir Luke, expecting this
audacious proposal, met it in a wonderfully dignified
manner.   Drawing himself up pompously, he frowned at

the unlucky Frank in a Jovian manner, and delivered himself of the following oration :

"Dr. Rebelspear, I am astonished—nay, thunderstruck, at the request you make. You are a young man, sir, with neither money nor position, and yet you have the boldness to demand from me the hand of my daughter in marriage. As you are, doubtless, aware, sir, she has been asked in marriage by many wealthy and titled gentlemen."

"Yes; and has refused them all because she loves me."

"Loves you ! loves you, sir ! " reiterated Sir Luke, turning as red as a turkey cock. "Pooh ! nonsense ! my daughter has, I trust, too much sense to encourage your ridiculous suit."

"Ridiculous ! " echoed Frank, flushing in his turn. "I see nothing ridiculous about it, Sir Luke, and I must beg of you to recall that word."

The baronet was proud and overbearing, but he was also just, and conscious that he had exceeded the bounds of courtesy, he at once withdrew the offensive epithet.

"I ask your pardon, Dr. Rebelspear, I did not mean to use the word ; but I am sure you will agree with me that it is hardly sensible for you to propose to keep a wife, when at present you cannot keep yourself."

"I will soon make a practice, Sir Luke."

"No doubt—no doubt—youth is always sanguine. Air castles are very fine things, Dr. Rebelspear, but unsubstantial, sir, very unsubstantial. You, I have no doubt, have a sufficiency of intellect, but what about patients, sir, —aye, that's the rub."

"I have one patient who came last night."

"Well, well, that is the first step. Still, one patient, however opulent, will not keep a doctor going."

"I'm afraid this first patient of mine is not very opulent," said Rebelspear, fixing his eyes steadily on the baronet; "on the contrary, he is very poor. No doubt you have heard of him, Sir Luke, as his name is Matthew Malister."

At the sound of this fatal name, Sir Luke grew very pale, and his right hand kept opening and shutting in a nervous manner; but beyond this, he gave no further signs of emotion. Rebelspear, having thus made the first attack, waited for Kernshaw to return or parry the blow, but the baronet seemed inclined to do neither one thing nor the other.

"Ah! Matthew Malister!" he said at last, with a visible effort; "is that not the madman who goes about talking of a coming plague?"

"The same. He was knocked over by a cab last night, and came to me to dress his wound."

"Have as little to do with him as possible, Rebelspear," said Sir Luke, vehemently; "he is a most dangerous character."

"You seem to know him very well, sir?" replied the young doctor, looking searchingly at the baronet.

The old man tried to meet that steady gaze, but was unable to do so, and after faltering forth a few words, relapsed into silence. Then recollecting that Rebelspear could not possibly know of his treachery towards Malister, he rose to his feet to intimate the interview was ended.

"I know nothing of this man," he said, coldly, "except

what I read in the papers. He seems to me to be one of
those mischievous persons who do a great deal of harm by
their fanaticism, and the wisest plan would be to shut him
up in some asylum."

"Which, no doubt, would be pleasing to you, Sir Luke."

"Dr. Rebelspear, what do you mean ?"

"I mean that I have heard Malister's story, and I
know, Sir Luke Kernshaw, that you are not what you
appear to be."

"You are mad!" gasped Sir Luke, with ashen looks.

"I am not mad ; I am as sane as you are. Malister told
me last night all about his false friend, his pretty wife, his
lost daughter ! Ah, you wince at those last words, Sir
Luke, and well you may, for you know that Malister's
daughter is not lost !"

"Not lost!"

"No ! she has been brought up as your own child—with
your own child, and either Laura or Eva, both of whom
the world calls your daughters, is the offspring of Matthew
Malister and not of Luke Kernshaw."

The baronet saw that his secret was known, and being
thus driven into a corner, he attempted to bully and bluster,
which was quite the wrong way to take with Frank
Rebelspear, as he soon saw.

"How dare you, sir ?" he cried, furiously, "how dare you
come here with such abominable lies ? You threaten me,
sir ; you dare to threaten me."

"I am not threatening you!" retorted Frank, springing to
his feet. "I came here to ask the hand of your daughter
Eva, whom I love, and you received me with insults. What

right have you to behave thus, sir? you whose past life holds this infamy of which I was told last night?"

"It's a lie! Malister is mad."

"Not in this matter. He is mad with religion, with fanaticism, mad about the destruction of London, about the coming plague, but what he says about you is true. You were his false friend, who robbed him of his wife and child, and one of these two girls who pass as your daughters is no kith nor kin of yours."

"Which of them is not my child?"

"I do not know!"

"No, Dr. Rebelspear, nor will you ever know. I deny all you have said, and as I have some influence with the Home Secretary I will have this Malister locked up as a madman. As for you, who come here to threaten me, I defy your threats, and I forbid you to speak or even see my daughter again."

"I shall do both, because I do not believe Eva is your daughter."

"Leave my house, sir, you—you medical pauper, or I will have you turned out by the servants."

"Sir Luke," said Frank, taking up his hat and gloves, "this interview is undignified and unworthy of us both. I did not come here to threaten you, but to ask permission to marry your daughter Eva!"

"I refuse the permission you ask."

"Very well! As I cannot obtain your permission one way I will do so in another. Malister has told me the truth about you I am sure, and I warn you, that I will leave no stone unturned to make the matter public."

" Threats again, sir ! "

" Call them what you like," replied Rebelspear, care-
lessly, going to the door. "But I love Eva, and she
loves me, so we are certainly not going to have our
lives spoilt by you, who I really believe have no right to
interfere."

" Not interfere with my own daughter ?" .

" Pardon me, Malister's daughter."

" You've got to prove that, Dr. Rebelspear."

" I will do so, Sir Luke, and within three days."

With this parting shot Frank took his departure, feeling
that if he had not secured a victory, he had, at least, sus-
tained a glorious defeat. He hardly liked the position he
had taken up, but the manner in which Sir Luke had met
his first courteous advances had left him no choice, and
now that he had declared war he determined to find out
the whole truth of the matter. If Eva proved to be the
daughter of Malister, he fully made up his mind to marry
her without delay, and if Sir Luke proved to be her father
he would secure his ends by some other means.

As he passed through the hall somewhat flushed after his
encounter with the baronet, he heard a light step behind
him and turned round quickly.

" Eva ! "

It was not Eva, however, but Laura, who flushed red
with anger when she heard the name of her sister.

" You expected to see Eva, and you are disappointed ,
only seeing me."

" Miss Kernshaw ! "

" Oh, I know why you have come here to-day," cried

Laura, tauntingly. "To ask my father's permission to marry Eva, and he has refused you."

"Yes!"

"I'm glad of it," she said, clenching her teeth. "You shall never marry Eva! a milk-and-water minx who is not worthy of you."

"Miss Kernshaw—your own sister!"

"My own sister," she said mockingly. "So you say—so the world says. But I— Do you know the habits of the cuckoo, Dr. Rebelspear, that leaves its young in a strange nest?"

"I cannot understand you, Miss Kernshaw."

"Can you not? Wait a little. You will understand shortly. What I know I know."

"But what do you know?"

"That you will never marry Eva!"

CHAPTER VII.

THE BURNING SICKNESS.

FOR many weeks an enormous comet had burned fiercely in the heavens, hanging over Europe like an avenging sword, to the great dismay of London's five million inhabitants. All the scientific men were perplexed over this comet which had appeared in a totally unexpected manner, and was evidently a new visitor to the solar system. The nucleus burned with a fierce dazzling light, and from it sprang two tails which swept in tremendous majesty across the whole expanse of the midnight sky. Even in the broad blaze of the sun the form of this tiger of the sky was perfectly visible, but at night the sight of the colossal visitor was truly appalling. Great was the discussion in scientific circles anent this comet, which some asserted to be a periodic one, identifying it with Halley's, which had last appeared in one thousand eight hundred and thirty-five, and which was due again about the beginning of the twentieth century. As this, however, was only the year nineteen hundred, and Halley's comet was calculated to be due in nineteen hundred and ten, it was hardly probable that it was the same, so this double-tailed monster was looked upon as new to the earth, or, at least, its last appearance had taken place in the dark ages when these visitors were regarded with the eye of superstition and not that of science.

At all events, new or old, the appearance of the comet made an extraordinary sensation, and many people, remembering the sign which had appeared in London prior to the Great Plague, believed the preaching of Malister when he asserted that this comet heralded a similar visitation. The believers in the prophecies of Daniel talked about the fulfilment of the appointed time, the creation of the kingdom of the beast, and looked upon this sign as one especially blazoned in the sky by God to mark the beginning of the great events about to take place. The greater number of the common people, however, believed in Malister, and his meetings in Hyde Park became quite a nuisance, owing to the multitudes which gathered to hear him. His incessant denunciations of the wickedness of London, his terrible prophecies of the coming plague, his frequent references to the great sword of light streaming in the sky, all began to have their effect, and a thrill of alarm ran through the mighty city. A wave of religion swept over the land, and the empty churches became filled with worshippers who strove to hide their uneasiness by devoutness of outward bearing. At last, the alarm became so general that the arrest of this new John the Baptist was ordered, but when the police attempted to seize him, he disappeared in the crowd with one last warning of the near approach of the Burning Sickness.

Two days afterwards the plague broke out.

It began in Whitechapel, that crowded centre of disease and crime, where several persons were seized by the sickness in the early morning, and during the day many more succumbed to this new malady, which the medical profession was quite unable to understand. The first symptoms were a slight feverishness, hot and cold chills, profuse perspiration, and swimming in the head like an attack of vertigo; then the whole body seemed to be consumed by some inward fire of the blood, and the victim, falling prone on the ground, was unable to move hand or foot, but gradually sank into a stupor, until released by death, which invariably took place within twelve hours after the first seizure.

From Whitechapel the plague spread to Stepney, where the mortality was very great; then with a sudden leap it passed over the city and appeared in Greenwich, far down the Thames. In vain the doctors tried to cope with this new disease; it defied all attempts to cure it, and when any one was seized the case was hopeless. The alarm of the people increased to a frenzy, and there was great danger of a riot taking place, owing to the terror felt by the inhabitants of the city. The streets in the lower parts of London were strewn with the dead and dying, while it took the undertakers all their time to bury the bodies.

To add to the horrors, every now and then Malister appeared in the affected districts, and preached fiercely against the wickedness of the age, taunting the people with neglecting his warnings, and glorying in their present calamity. Furious at these insults, the mob would have killed Malister, but he always managed to evade them and vanished for a time, only to reappear in a new part of London at some fresh outbreak of the Burning Sickness.

The papers, of course, were full of the matter, and regarded it as merely a local visitation which would soon pass; but the authorities could not conceal the alarm which they felt at the magnitude of the disaster. All the medical profession in London met together in order to consult as to the best way of curing this new disease, but they were unable to come to any decision and separated in confusion, all of which, being reported in the papers, increased the terrors felt by the overcrowded population.

Dr. Rebelspear, on hearing of the outbreak of a new disease in Whitechapel, did not pay much attention to it, still disbelieving in the wild story told by Malister; but when he heard how rapidly the disease was spreading, and how its appearance in a fresh place was always heralded by the preaching of the fanatic, he began to think that there might be some truth in the story after all.

For some time he tried to find Malister, but was unable to do so, as a constant dread of the police kept the fanatic away from the West End, and he always appeared in the most unexpected places; so that Frank might as well have attempted to catch a will-o'-the-wisp as this extraordinary creature, whose very appearance was hailed as fatal. The young doctor, now seriously alarmed about the affair, hastened to Park Lane to see Sir Luke, and implore him to leave London with his daughters, but the baronet would not grant him an interview, and Frank was forced to return to his own house in a very disturbed state of mind.

After his interview with Sir Luke, he had not been permitted to see Eva, nor even to correspond with her, and now that this terrible disease was devastating the East End, he trembled lest it should make its appearance in Park

Lane and kill the girl he loved before he could save her.

Save her? Yes, he felt sure that he could save her, for had he not in his possession the phial given to him by the old fanatic? Formerly he had disbelieved in its virtues, but now that the plague, foretold by Malister, had actually arrived, Rebelspear, seeing that one part of the story was true, did not see why he should not believe the other. He had no doubt that Malister had broken the phial, containing the germs of the plague, in Whitechapel, from which nucleus the disease was now spreading all over London, and believing this—which he could hardly help doing now—he was quite satisfied that the contents of the phial in his desk would cure the Burning Sickness.

When the meeting of doctors took place in order to see whether they could find a remedy for this strange disease, Rebelspear was very nearly attending it and telling his story about Malister and the phial. But after some little reflection he determined to keep silent, at least, for some time, as he was afraid lest his *confrères* should treat his narrative as an absurdity, and all he would gain would be contempt and scorn. With this idea in his head, he kept silent about the cure, but nevertheless he took it out of his desk to examine it.

Remembering the instructions of Malister, he half filled a glass with water, and, unscrewing the glass stopper of the phial, he found that it contained a clear, colourless liquid, thick and oily like glycerine. With great care he dropped three drops of this sluggish liquid into the water, upon which the contents of the glass assumed a purplish tinge, and in another minute changed to a deep crimson. Rebel-spear smelt this preparation, which had a pungent odour, like ammonia, and having tasted it, also discovered that the flavour was intensely bitter. What it was he could not determine, as although he analysed it with the greatest care he was quite unable to come to any conclusion regarding its component parts. If it cured, as Malister said, every drop was worth its weight in gold, therefore Rebel-spear felt a great desire to try its effects upon some person afflicted with the Burning Sickness. No one was at hand, however, as the disease had not yet reached the West End, so Rebelspear replaced the phial in his desk and put the tumbler, containing the blood-red water, into a small cabinet near the window.

"At all events," he said to himself, when this was done, "if this Burning Sickness does seize me, I shall be able to cure myself and Eva also."

But Eva! ah, how he wished that he could see her and tell her of the cure he had in his possession, but Sir Luke was still resentful against him for the way he had spoken to him, and Rebelspear was shut out from Paradise. He tried to see Eva at balls—at times in the Park; but she was always accompanied by Laura, who refused to let her sister speak to the man whom she loved herself.

Of one thing Rebelspear was certain: that Laura knew one of them was not the child of Sir Luke, and, moreover, knew which one it was. Her words to him in the hall of the Park Lane mansion indicated Eva, but it was possible that she herself might be the child of Malister. The only way of finding out would be to have another conversation with

Malister, but he had not been near the young doctor since that fatal night when he had revealed such horrors.

Julian Delicker had also left town, and would doubtless keep away now that he heard of the plague. Frank could hardly help wondering how he regarded the outbreak of the disease after all his scoffings at the prophecies of Malister, but, no matter what view he took of the affair, Rebelspear was satisfied that he would look after himself and keep away from danger.

There was thus no one to whom Frank could speak about his fears for Eva, or of the mystery which involved the birth of the sisters, so he mostly stayed at home, still waiting for patients, and worrying over his enforced separation from the girl he loved.

Not knowing he had a cure for the plague, no one came to see him, and he was as far off making a beginning in his profession as ever. True, he might advertise that he could cure the Burning Sickness, but then he would be simply overwhelmed with patients, and the contents of the phial was so precious that if he exhausted it in curing for gold he might himself fall a victim to the disease itself, in which case his money would be of no use to him. Besides, he felt sure that the disease would yet come to the West End, and Eva would fall a victim, so he carefully hoarded that precious phial that he might help her and himself in time of need. Up to the present, however, the disease had not visited Belgravia, and the upper ten did not regard the plague in the East End as serious. They were sorry certainly, but they did not think it would attack them, so went on gaily with their usual amusements without thinking of the terrible spectre that was at their doors.

They sang, they danced, they feasted, they sinned, nor dreamed that the Angel of Death was hovering over them; but the handwriting was on the wall, and the days of their wickedness, their luxury, and their idleness were drawing to a close.

CHAPTER VIII.

THREE DROPS IN A GLASS OF WATER.

It was now about a week since the Burning Sickness had first made its appearance, and during that time it had steadily increased. Every day the number of victims grew larger, and aided, doubtless, by the dry heat of summer, the disease was spreading with rapid virulence. As yet, however, it was confined to the poorer parts of the city, and every effort was made to prevent its penetrating to the West End. Large bonfires were lighted in the streets in the hope of destroying the germs in the air; all persons were strictly forbidden to leave the infected districts, and all that human ingenuity could devise was done in order to check the progress of the pestilence, but without result, for at the end of a fortnight from its first appearance the Burning Sickness made its appearance in Park Lane.

As usual it was headed by Malister, who suddenly re-appeared on Sunday morning in Hyde Park, and delivered a short, fiery speech, in which he told the well-dressed idlers that all their precautions were vain; then, before he could be seized, he darted off rapidly through the Park by Achille's Statue. Many of the police started off after him, but in spite of his great age the old man was wonderfully fleet of foot, and dodged, and twisted, and turned, and doubled until his pursuers were fairly out of breath. In spite of his nimbleness, however, he would, doubtless, in the end, have been captured, had he not suddenly vaulted on to a horse which was fastened to an iron pillar on the curb stone, and cutting the reins loose, started off full speed down Oxford Street, crying: "The plague! the plague!"

The police, being on foot, were unable to keep up with him, and thus having a good start Malister was regarded as a herald of the plague, which inspired such dread in the crowd that no one attempted to stop him. At length he disappeared down a side street, and the people were left looking apprehensively at one another, wondering whether the pestilence was really in their midst.

It was a hot, burning, summer day, with a cloudless sky, and being Sunday everyone was dressed in his or her gayest apparel, when suddenly a young man in the crowd, who had been shivering as with ague for some time, threw up his hands with a loud cry and fell prone on the earth. That cry sent an electric thrill through the multitude, and everyone hastened home in a frenzy of alarm. The authorities took as prompt steps as possible, and the young man who had been seized with the Burning Sickness was at once removed; but the Monday morning papers were full of the affair, and everyone knew that the much-dreaded pestilence was at last in the West End.

Dr. Rebelspear was horrified when he heard of the terrible event which had happened in Oxford Street, and he made up his mind to swallow his pride and go once more to the house in Park Lane in order to implore Sir Luke to take his daughters out of town. Crowds of people were already leaving London, but Sir Luke, being confined to his house with gout, had not yet left the neighbourhood, and, with characteristic selfishness, he refused to let either Laura or Eva go. At any moment one of the three might be seized with the plague, and then, unless he was at hand to administer the cure, Frank felt sure that he would lose the girl he loved.

Going to his desk he took thence the phial, so as to be prepared for emergencies, and, putting on his hat, was about to start for Kernshaw's house, when the door of his study was violently thrown open, and Julian Delicker rushed—or rather reeled—into the room.

Yes, it was Julian Delicker, pale and haggard, with his usually neat attire all in disorder; and as Rebelspear looked at him in astonishment he saw that the unfortunate young man was shaking as with ague.

"Julian !" he cried, as his old schoolfellow fell into a chair in a state of exhaustion ; "what is the matter? Good God ! have you—"

"The cure ! the cure !" gasped Julian, feverishly ; "give me the phial that Malister gave you. I have the plague."

"The plague !"

"Yes ! Do you remember how I scoffed and laughed at the old man, Frank? God forgive me. It is true, perfectly true, all he said. He has brought this devil-curse with him from Arabia, and soon there will not be one person left alive in this city."

"But I thought you were out of town?"

"I was! I was down at Brighton, but the plague is there!"

"At Brighton! impossible."

"I tell you it is true. It is spreading all over the kingdom, while, as for London, thousands are dying every day."

"Poor Eva!"

"Eva, Eva!" cried Delicker, with a ghastly laugh, "don't talk about her, Frank. Is this the time to marry and talk of love in this carnival of death? Give me the cure or I shall die! You have that phial, have you not?"

"Yes; here it is!"

Delicker uttered a cry of joy, and stretched his hands out towards the glittering crystal.

"Thank God, thank God! I shall live, I shall live. O, Frank, if you only knew the tortures I have endured. I was seized with this cursed Sickness down at Brighton, and I came up by the next train to see you, the only man who I knew could cure me. Give me the cure, quick; quick, I may fall down any moment."

"Wait," said Rebelspear, filling a glass with water; "I must prepare it as old Malister told me. The old villain! he ought to be hanged for inflicting this terrible disease on London."

"If I meet him I'll kill him, Frank. I will, I will! Do you know that my mother is dead of this cursed plague? My friends are dying daily, and I—every moment I feel that I am getting nearer to death."

"Tell me how you feel."

"How can I tell? I am hot and cold by turns—then my blood seems to be on fire. My head swims round and round—oh, it is terrible ! Have you seen anyone die of this Burning Sickness, Frank ?"

"Yes ; many !"

"And you never saved them ?"

"How could I ?" replied Frank, dropping the three drops into the glass of water ; "there is not enough in this phial to save more than a few people. If I had done so I would not have been able to save you."

"You believe it will act ?"

"I don't know, but as one part of Malister's story is true, I don't see why the other should not be. See, the water is crimson as he described. Drink it at once and we will see if it will cure you."

"It must, it must, I cannot die now. I am too young to die."

He stretched out his hands eagerly towards the glass, rising to his feet in his intense desire to seize the life-giving draught—when, just as his fingers touched it, he gave a wild shriek and fell like a log on the floor.

There he lay paralysed in every limb, unable to move hand or foot, with a look of agony on his worn face, and an incessant cry for that precious glass of crimson fluid which would bring him back again from the grave.

"Frank, Frank ! I can't move, I can't move ! I'm all on fire within. Dear old fellow, give me the drink and save me. You don't want to see me die before your eyes, do you ?"

"No ! no, of course not," answered Frank, kneeling down beside this helpless log of humanity. "Here, drink this up at once."

"Where is it?" moaned Julian, feebly. "I can't see it, there is a mist before my eyes. I feel dull and stupid. Ah!"

His last ejaculation was caused by his dry lips coming in contact with the rim of the glass, and with greedy avidity he drank down every drop that was in the tumbler.

"Dear old fellow! Good old Frank!" he murmured, drowsily; "that does me good. It cools my blood; but, oh, Frank, do you think I am going to die?"

"No, no! I am sure this will cure you, Julian."

"Give me your hand, Frank; I'm afraid to be alone. Oh, what a coward I am!"

"Let me put you on the couch first," said Rebelspear, and lifting Julian in his arms he laid him gently on the sofa.

"Your hand; I'm afraid. Give me your hand," muttered Julian, thickly, and then his eyes closed and he sank into a profound slumber, while Frank sat patiently by his side holding his hand.

The windows of the consulting-room were wide open and the hot air flowed into the room. Through the luminous haze Frank could see the spires of the churches and the tops of the near houses, but the familiar sounds of traffic and human voices were missing. Not the roll of a wheel or the cry of a man broke the intense silence, and Frank saw how truly Malister had spoken when he said that this mighty London would become as desolate and deserted as the sand-girdled city of Nar.

Hour after hour passed slowly, and Rebelspear began to feel somewhat cramped as he sat there with his hand tightly clutched by Julian. He was unwilling to remove it, being afraid lest any disturbing influence should interfere with the cure; so there he sat through the long afternoon watching the face of the sleeping man. After an hour or so had passed, the dazed look vanished from the countenance of the patient, and a calm, sleeping look appeared instead; then drops of moisture began to gather on his forehead, the hand which Frank held became damp, and in a short time it became evident that Julian was bathed from head to foot in profuse perspiration. His breathing was calm and regular, the burning heat seemed to have passed away, and when the clock in the adjacent church sounded six, he awoke with a smile of gratitude on his face, after having slept five hours.

"How do you feel, Julian?" asked Rebelspear, rising to his feet and stretching his cramped limbs.

"I feel splendid! All the burning feeling has passed away. My head is perfectly clear; and oh, Frank, I feel so fearfully hungry."

"That's a good sign anyhow," said Frank, ringing the bell for the servant to bring up food.

"What have you been doing, Frank?"

"Sitting by you, holding your hand."

Julian slowly got off the couch, and rising to his feet walked across the room to his friend.

"Frank," he said in a tone of emotion, "words are idle to express what I feel to you for saving my life, but I hope some day to show my gratitude."

"Don't thank me, Julian, but rather God, for having saved you."

"I do thank Him, and most fervently! But oh, Frank, this cure is true after all."

"It appears so."

"Then let us get Eva Kernshaw and leave this cursed city at once."

"But the money?"

"I have plenty, and whatever I have is yours."

"Still—"

"Not a word, Frank Rebelspear. You have saved my life. Nothing I can do for you can ever repay that. We will go to the Continent, and you will marry Eva at once."

"But her father?"

"Sir Luke? Oh, he deserves to die, for had it not been for his treachery, Malister would never have gone to Arabia and brought back this terrible pestilence."

CHAPTER IX.

THE SPREAD OF THE PLAGUE.

OWING to the Burning Sickness the season of one thousand nine hundred had abruptly come to an end; and everyone who could possibly manage to do so was flying from the fated city. Many wanted to go to the Continent, but so great was the dread there of the plague that the dwellers on the mainland refused to allow the fugitives to land on their shores. The steamers across the English Channel stopped running; and no English person was allowed to set foot in France or Belgium. In America, too, the same selfish fear prevailed, and the United States refused to hold any communication with England whatsoever. The whole of the United Kingdom was boycotted by the world; and to the horrors of the plague there seemed likely to be added the still more appalling horrors of famine.

Of course, owing to the blockade, neither Julian nor Frank Rebelspear could cross over to the Continent; and even had they been able to do so, Eva Kernshaw would not have fled with them, not even with the man she loved.

2 C

Sir Luke was still confined to his house with gout, and was unable to leave London owing to the difficulty found in obtaining means of transport, besides which it was simply a case of "out of the frying pan into the fire," as the Burning Sickness had spread throughout the whole of the three kingdoms. In Liverpool, Manchester, Dublin, Glasgow, and Edinburgh the mortality was something frightful; while as for the capital itself the people were dying in the streets like dogs, at the rate of hundreds a day. The Government had almost given up even the semblance of authority, as they had hardly any men with whom to work; and the army, the police, the officials of all grades were thoroughly demoralised owing to the frightful state of things.

All through those hot July days the plague steadily increased, and the task of burying the dead was now quite beyond the power of the living. All the shops were shut up; whole streets were deserted, and grass actually began to grow in some of them. Of course not a theatre was open, as there were neither actors to act nor audiences to attend, and the people thronged the churches in countless numbers. All these old city churches, built after the Great Fire of 1666, and so long left to silence and dust, were now crowded with frantic people trying to avert the wrath of heaven with useless prayers.

This was the boasted age of science, when all the worms of the earth denied the existence of God; and lo! now that He had smitten them in His wrath, they were on their knees imploring Him to spare them. In this trying time the clergy came nobly to the front, and worked night and day among the dying—helping, succouring, aiding, consoling their unhappy fellow-creatures. The streets were cumbered with the dead and the dying. Trafalgar Square was one great sepulchre—hardly a cab, a cart, or a horse was to be seen on the streets, and a silence reigned over the whole of this mighty city, only broken by the wailing of those seized by the mortal Sickness. It seemed as if London was doomed, as if every man, woman, and child would perish under this terrible scourge of God; and over all the frightful desolation and terror still hung that fierce comet flaming in the cloudless sky like the visible sword of the Angel of Death.

Frank tried to see Sir Luke and Eva in order to help them, but the old baronet had barricaded himself in his house in dread of the plague; and he, his daughters, and his servants were shut up as in a tomb. Longing for news of the woman he loved, Frank used to wander up and down in front of the house calling upon Eva, but she never came, and he thought that in her dread of the pestilence she had forgotten him. In all his wanderings, Rebelspear was accompanied by Julian; and many a time would have saved some poor wretch by that wonderful phial had not Delicker warned him that there was but enough to save himself and Eva. This stayed his hand, and he was forced to see his fellow-men dying on all sides without being able to save them from death.

After seeing how Julian was cured, however, something appeared to him to be necessary to stay the disease, and that was to induce profuse perspiration which sweated out all the humours of the sickness. He suggested this remedy to several physicians, and it was immediately tried with great success, so at last there seemed to be some chance of stopping the plague.

"Julian," said Frank, one day, after they had been working hard at helping the sick and the dying, "I wonder what has become of old Malister?"

"The last time I heard of him, he was preaching at St. Paul's," replied Julian. "Why, what do you want to see him about?"

"I want to find out whether there is any chance of stopping this plague. He possibly may know of some remedy."

"I doubt it!"

"However, we can but try; besides, I want to discover the truth about those two girls, so let us go to St. Paul's this evening and find him if possible."

This being settled, they went off immediately after dinner; a very meagre dinner it was, as provisions were now frightfully dear, owing to the blockade. It seemed as if the rest of the world were going to let the English die of hunger, and had it not been for the fleet, without doubt things would have been much worse. The Americans, however, sent over many ships laden with grain and cattle, and the Continental nations also did their best; so if there was not plenty, there was at least enough to keep people alive. Julian and Frank, however, were too anxious-minded to eat much, and after having lighted their pipes as a preventive against infection, they started off for the city.

Of course it was impossible to get a vehicle of any sort,

so they had to walk the whole way, and all along the Strand found themselves impeded by dead bodies, which were being gathered into closed carts and taken to the great pits dug outside the city.

" Does not this put you in mind of Defoe, Julian?" said Frank, as they saw cart after cart with its dolorous burden moving off. " Bring out your dead! Bring out your dead!"

" Yes, and this is more frightful than the last plague as the population is so much larger."

" They ought to bury those corpses as quickly as possible, for with the present heat things will come to a frightful pitch if they are left unburied. Did you see Trafalgar Square as we came past—pah! like one vast charnel house. See, there go some of the Life Guards. I wonder what is up?"

" I know," said Julian, after a pause. " Malister is stirring up all sorts of rows with his preaching, and they are going to arrest him."

" All those soldiers to arrest one man! Absurd."

" Not one man! Malister is supported by the populace, who believe him to be a prophet. Fancy that in our days, Frank! I expect there will be a row."

The soldiers moved quickly down the Strand at a sharp trot, with the rays of the sunset flashing on their glittering arms and accoutrements, while the jingling of their martial panoply sounded clear and distinct through the stillness.

" It looks like the sacking of a city," said Frank, as they quickly followed the troops, " these closed houses, these dead bodies, and the soldiers riding along. I can hardly believe that this is London."

"It is no longer London!" replied Julian, with some sadness. "It will never be London again."

"Ah, you think so now; but what about your idea of a plague for the regeneration of mankind?"

"Oh!" cried Julian, with a shudder, "all my ideas vanish before this terrible reality; but, hark! there are the first mutterings of the storm."

A low hoarse murmur like the sound of waves breaking upon a lonely beach announced the vicinity of the crowd. By this time the two friends had arrived at Ludgate Hill, just under the railway arch, and looking up the street they saw that the space in front of the Cathedral was filled with a great multitude, and the troop of soldiers were drawn across the upper end of the street. As they walked up to the square they saw that Malister had climbed up on the pedestal of Queen Anne's statue, and could hear his voice harsh and vehement ringing through the air.

"Woe! woe! woe! to the wicked city—to the evil city that hath sat proudly with the princes of the earth. Her towers shall be cast down, her pride shall be humbled in the dust. The arm of the Lord is stretched out in His might, and none shall escape from His wrath. But a portion of your trouble is come unto you, oh city of palaces, and the days of your mourning are not yet completed! Woe! woe! woe! for the sword of the Lord is in the heavens and it hath smitten the children of men."

Behind him arose the immense façade of the Cathedral, with its great doors and many windows and figures of saints, while high above, the mighty dome rose into the clear sky like a huge bubble, bearing on its summit the golden cross, symbol of Christianity; but higher than the dome, higher than the cross, flashed the comet, with terrible splendour, in the heavens.

The crowd below swayed hither and thither, with murmurs, as the fierce denunciations of Malister sounded through the square, and then turned boldly on the little troop of soldiers. The Riot Act was read, commanding them to disperse; but, encouraged by Malister, they refused to do so, and the captain gave orders to charge. For one moment there was a dead silence, and then the military and the crowd closed in deadly conflict. Shrieks, oaths, cries, shots; it was a perfect babel of sounds, as the soldiers rode down the poor wretches before them, trying to cut a path to Malister, who still stood tossing his arms, upon the pedestal of the statue. Julian had fought his way, in company with Frank, nearly to this point, when he heard the officer give the order to fire, and he had just time to pull his friend down before a volley rang out, and Malister fell wounded from the pedestal.

Frank was close to him, and took him by the arm, but the fanatic was only slightly hurt in one of his arms, and, with a cry of rage, he tore himself from the grasp of the young man, and vanished in the crowd.

On seeing the fall of their prophet, the crowd, not having any further courage for fighting, began to melt away; and with them disappeared Malister, who could not be found, so the guard rode back to Whitehall, in some disgust at their bad fortune; while Julian and Frank returned home.

CHAPTER X.

RIVALS.

A FEW days after the riot at St. Paul's Cathedral, Frank was sitting alone in his consulting-room, plunged in gloomy reflections. Julian had gone in search of Malister, who, rumour asserted, had taken up his abode in one of the deserted mansions in Park Lane; so Frank was left quite alone with his own thoughts, which were none of the pleasantest. He had heard nothing of Eva for many days, and for all he knew, she might be already dead, while the terrible calamity which had befallen the English nation, and the disorganisation of the country, promised but a gloomy future for many years to come.

While sitting in this unenviable frame of mind, the door opened slowly, and Eva herself walked into the room. She was dressed in some soft, grey material, and wore a thin, grey veil, which she flung back as she came towards her lover, showing her face, pale and worn-looking, with dark circles under her eyes, and a pinched look about her lips.

"Frank!" she cried, joyfully, throwing herself into his arms, "my dearest! how glad I am to see you again."

"Eva!" he replied, covering her face with kisses, "what are you doing here?"

"I came to see you."

"But your father?"

"O, Frank, my father!" she answered, bursting into tears, "he is ill, Frank; terribly ill with the Burning Sickness."

"Sir Luke seized with the plague! Since when?"

"This morning. After breakfast he began to shiver terribly, and had to return to bed, so bad did he feel. Oh! it is the plague, Frank,—this fearful plague! All the servants have left the house."

. "But Laura?"

"She is with papa, looking after him, and when they were in the bedroom together I ran out of the house to see you."

"My darling! if you only knew how I have longed for a sight of your dear face. But you look ill and worn, Eva! Great Heavens! you have not the plague?"

"No! no! not yet, but I shall have it; I know I shall have it soon, and then I shall die."

"My dear Eva, you will not die!"

"How so? There is no cure for this disease."

"Yes, there is, and I have the cure!"

"Frank!"

She gave a cry of joy, and clung frantically round his neck in the revulsion of feeling she experienced in hearing that there was a chance of escaping this dreaded pestilence. The suspense, the anxiety, the dread, had all been too much for her delicate constitution, and Frank found, to his dismay, that she had fainted.

"Poor girl!" he said to himself, as he rang the bell for the servant, and placed her inanimate form on the sofa. "I don't wonder that she is worn out with all this trouble."

When the servant appeared, Frank ordered him to bring up some wine, and when this was done, filled a glass for Eva. The servant paused for a moment at the door.

"I beg pardon, sir, but it ain't the plague?"

"No! Miss Kernshaw has only fainted. If it were the plague I suppose you'd run away, Philips?"

Philips did not reply to this, but the expression of his face plainly said that such was his intention.

"More fool you if you did," said Frank, coolly sprinkling the face of Eva with water. "There's no place for you to go to, and if you are seized by the Burning Sickness while you are with me, I may perhaps cure you."

Philips looked dubious at this, and retired slowly shaking his head, while Frank, after some trouble, managed to revive the girl.

"Come, Eva, dear," he said, holding the glass to her lips. "Take a little of this port wine and you will be all right."

"No! no!"

"Yes! yes! remember I am your doctor now, as well as your lover, and you must do as I bid you."

Thus adjured, Eva drank the wine, and the generous liquor soon sent a glow of heat through her slender frame. Sitting up, she dried her eyes, and leaning on her lover's shoulder, began to talk quickly.

"Frank ! you say you can cure the plague."

"I can."

"Then cure my father."

At this Frank looked somewhat doubtful, as there was only enough in the phial to cure two people, and these he intended to be himself and Eva.

"I'm afraid I have not enough of the cure," he said at last in a hesitating manner. "If I am ill I want to cure myself, and if you are seized with the plague I want to cure you."

"But poor papa, Frank ; oh, you must cure poor papa."

"Then one of us must die," said Frank, gravely, going to his desk. "See here, Eva, in this little phial there is a liquid which will cure the plague, but there is just enough left for you and me. If I could I would obtain some more ; but, unfortunately, I cannot find the man who gave me this cure. If I cure your father there will only be enough left for you, and if I am seized with the Burning Sickness I must die."

"Oh, no, Frank ; you will not die. Cure papa and keep the rest of the cure for yourself. I will die, not you."

"Then what will life be to me without you ?"

"You will find someone else to love."

"Never, Eva ! You are the only woman I shall ever love."

"But Laura loves you."

"Impossible, my dear Eva," said Rebelspear, flushing with vexation. "Laura knows I am engaged to you ; that I love you only."

"I know she does, Frank ; and it is that which makes her so severe with me. Since she has known that she has not been like a sister to me,"

"Then be my wife, Eva; and we will defy both your sister and your father."

"But I cannot be your wife in this terrible time."

"Yes, you can! I will find a clergyman to marry us, and then we will try to go to America or the Continent."

"But you have no money, Frank."

"Yes, I have. Julian will give me what I want. You know I saved his life."

"Then save papa's, Frank!" cried Eva, returning to her first idea. "Do promise to save papa's life."

"At the risk of my own?"

"No! at the risk of mine!"

"Impossible!"

"Frank, on my knees I implore you to do so. Think of my father lying on his death-bed and you can save him, yet will not. Oh, Frank, you have a kind heart! Papa has been cruel to you I know, but you will save him, Frank! Promise me you will."

Poor Rebelspear was in a terrible dilemma. If he saved Sir Luke, one of them must be sacrificed. He certainly would not let Eva die, and yet he did not want to die himself. At last he thought he would try the effect of one drop upon Sir Luke, which perhaps might cure him. If it did, there would be enough left for himself and Eva, but if it did not cure, Eva could not but believe he had done his best to help her father. With this idea in his mind he raised the weeping girl from the floor and kissed her fondly.

"Dry your eyes, my dearest; I will cure your father."

" Oh, my dear, dear Frank ! "

She bowed her head on his shoulder, weeping tears of joy, while Frank soothed her fondly with all those endearments in which lovers delight. Just as they were in this position they heard a sneering laugh, and both looked up to see Laura Kernshaw standing at the door.

Rebelspear had once seen a picture of a famous actress as Lady Macbeth, waiting for her husband while he murdered Duncan, and he was struck by the resemblance which Laura now bore to the picture. Her beautiful face bore the impress of a vengeful look, and arrayed in a long black cloak, with a scarlet ribbon at her throat, and a savage look in her eyes, she appeared to be a very dangerous woman.

" A pretty tableau indeed," she cried, with a jeering laugh; " so this is where you are, Eva ? I thought as much. Your father is dying, yet from his death-bed you come to the arms of your lover."

" Oh ! " cried Eva, hiding her face with shame at the idea, " what a cruel, cruel thing to say."

" Nevertheless it is true ! " retorted Laura, coming close to the pair ; " deny it if you can."

" I do deny it. What you say is false."

" So you say, I have no doubt. But it is true."

" It is not," cried Frank, who had hitherto kept silence. " Eva came to me to ask if I could cure her father."

" A very good excuse, Dr. Rebelspear, but one that will hardly serve with me. You cannot cure the Burning Sickness."

" I can and will."

"Pardon me if I doubt you!"

Frank darted a look of indignation at her, and pointed to the phial which was lying on his desk.

"That phial contains the cure," he said, slowly; "three drops in a glass of water will save anyone from this plague, and I am now going with Eva to your father in order to cure him."

"I don't believe you."

"That is as you please, Miss Kernshaw; but I cured Mr. Delicker with it."

Laura looked longingly at the phial as if she would like to test the truth of his assertion, and then turned savagely upon her sister.

"Do you believe this story, Eva?"

"I do! I believe anything that Frank tells me."

"How blindly in love you are," retorted Laura, biting her lips; "however, as I am not so simple, I decline to believe in the virtues of this elixir until I see it put to the test. Meantime, perhaps you will come with me back to our father's bedside. Dr. Rebelspear can come if he likes."

"And he certainly does like," said Frank, boldly.

Laura stamped her foot with rage, and without taking any more notice of Frank, advanced towards her sister, whom she seized roughly by the arm.

"Come at once!"

Eva uttered a cry of pain, upon which Frank, who was putting on his hat, turned round quickly and drew her away from the beautiful fury.

"I myself will take charge of Eva," he said, leading the

girl to the door. "You can follow, Miss Kernshaw, if you like."

Thus mockingly repeating her own words, he left the room with Eva on his arm, and Laura was left alone by the desk, with a look of impotent fury marring her face.

"Oh!" she hissed between her clenched teeth, "if I could only kill them both! If they could be stricken by the pestilence, and die at my feet, how happy I should be."

Meanwhile, Frank and Eva were walking slowly along. He was trying to console the sobbing girl who was terribly upset by the way in which her sister had treated her.

"It's jealousy, Frank, jealousy! she cannot bear to see us happy together."

"Never mind, Eva," he replied, soothingly, "I will marry you after I have cured your father. Oh!"

"What is the matter?"

"I have left the phial behind, so I must go back for it. Wait here, Eva, I will return in a few minutes."

He ran back hastily to his consulting-room and found Laura just at the door evidently leaving the house. When she saw him, a flush of joy passed over her face, and she laid her hand on his arm.

"Frank!" she said, imploringly. "Frank, have you come back for me?"

"For you?" he repeated indignantly; "no, I have come back for that phial containing the cure."

Brushing hastily past her, he went into the room, and picking up the phial, which was still lying on the desk, slipped it into his pocket. Laura stood where he had left her, biting her under lip; and as he came out of the room, once more detained him.

"Then you do not love me?"

"No," he said, with a gesture of aversion, "I love your sister."

CHAPTER XI.

NEMESIS.

"As ye have sown so shall ye reap," came true enough to Sir Luke Kernshaw, as he found out by bitter experience, for this comparatively early death was the outcome of his youthful follies. Had he not deeply wronged his old friend by robbing him of his wife, Malister would not have gone to the East, and had he not gone to the East he would not have brought to London this terrible disease whereof his enemy was now dying; therefore, by the irony of fate, Kernshaw had, so to speak, brought himself to this pass by his own acts. There he lay, the unhappy man, an immovable log on his gorgeous bed in a darkened room, with the fearful Sickness burning in his every vein, unable to turn to the right or the left, but compelled to lie like Dives amid the torments of hell.

The disease had made considerable progress in a short space of time, owing to his enfeebled body, and although speech was still left to him, yet even that was now becoming thick and indistinct. All the servants had fled in terror from the house at the first whisper of the plague, his daughters had both disappeared, and Kernshaw lay in agony, apparently deserted by God and man.

92

All around him spoke of wealth : the rich carpets soft to the foot and pleasant to the eye, the delicately tinted hangings, the thousand and one objects of art and luxury which filled the chamber. All these met his languid eye as he stared vaguely through the semi-twilight of the room. He was rich, he was lying amid his riches, yet they could not save him. No! the Burning Sickness had him in its fatal grip, and every breath of the warm summer air wafted in through the windows was impregnated with the venom of the plague, while he, robbed of all motion by the distemper, could not rise and flee from this splendid sepulchre.

Lying there with a feeling as if he were wrapped in burning flames, Kernshaw, staring through the dim twilight, saw as in a dream all the events of his past life rise up before him, and Conscience, cruel showman to this wild phantasmagoria, sat by his pillow, explaining each event that pictured itself on the thin air.

"Do you remember those days," whispered Conscience, as two merry lads appeared, "schoolfellows, both—are they not happy? Do they not love one another? They are to be friends for life, you know. The Orestes and Pylades of modern days. Do you remember them ? "

"Too well, too well," groaned Sir Luke, in bitter anguish.

"See now, they are both grown up, and still their friendship in the world is as true as their friendship at school. Now, one of them goes awooing—is it you or your boy friend? You know best. Do you see the fair wife that your friend has won? Yes, you do. They live in paradise, and you, O serpent! masking your lust under the guise of friendship, watch for an opportunity to destroy that paradise."

" No more! oh, no more!"

"See how you come like a thief in the night," pursues Conscience, relentlessly, "and steal away your friend's wife. You are happy for a time, but behold the wages of sin. Ah, yes, she died in your arms, and the child is left with you to guard it. This is the one good deed of your life: you save the child. And now, see yourself rich, married, happy with a fair wife and child. All is well with you as the world thinks, but for many a year I have sat, as I sit now, whispering to you of your evil past."

"Forgive me."

"No one can forgive you but the man whom you have wronged. See, here he comes, old, frail, broken down—your work. That eye once beaming with sanity now gleams with the fire of madness—your work. Fallen, despised, hated, feared—all your work."

"Malister!"

Was it indeed Malister who stood silently upon the threshold of the chamber of death, with a look of triumph in his wild eyes—or still the phantom of his imagination conjured up by Conscience? No, it was Malister in flesh and blood! Malister the fanatic! Malister the avenger! Malister the madman, who had now come to gloat over the victim whom his hand had stricken thus to the dust!

With terrified eyes Kernshaw saw the fanatic approach his couch, and stand over him with folded arms. He was completely at the mercy of the man whom he had wronged.

Chained to his bed by the fever, paralysed by the plague, without power to move hand or foot, with hardly the capability to articulate a word, he lay there prostrate under the eye of his enemy waiting—waiting for his punishment.

"So, Luke," said Malister, in his deep harsh tones, "this is the end of all your wickedness. 'The wages of sin is death!' Ah! you know it now—now that the world you loved is passing away from you. Ho! Dives, do you not already in your body feel the torments of hell?"

"Mercy, mercy!"

"Such mercy as you gave to me I bestow upon you. I was happy, and you destroyed my happiness. 1 trusted you, and you betrayed me. I loved my wife, and you stole her from me. I had a dear little daughter, you took her away. Traitor! liar! dastard!—where is my lost happiness — where is my wife — where is my child? Answer!"

The pale lips of the dying man made some movement, but the keen ears of Malister could detect no sound. Filled with fury at the sight of his enemy, all the repressed rancour of years swelled in his breast, and he shook the dying man violently with a jeer on his furious lips.

"Liar! traitor! answer! My happiness is lost—I know that. My wife is dead, as you soon will be, I trust; but my child — what about my child, you perjured traitor?"

"Lives," whispered Sir Luke, with a great effort.

"My child lives, she lives!" cried Malister in a tone of joy, "where is she? where is she?"

"There!"

As the words fell reluctantly from his hot dry lips, his eyes turned towards the door of the room, and there on the threshold stood two women—both young, both beautiful—but one was as fair as the day—the other as dark as the night.

"My daughter, my daughter," cried Malister, rushing towards them with outstretched arms, "which of you is my daughter?"

Both the girls looked at this strange being in silent surprise—looked past him to the silent figure lying on the bed as if seeking for an explanation, and there was a dead silence for a moment, broken suddenly by a cry of triumph as Dr. Rebelspear sprang forward to confront the man for whom he had sought so long in vain.

"Malister!" he cried, seizing the fanatic by the wrist. "Fiend! demon that you are! can you not stay this plague which you have created?"

"No! My mission is to destroy, not to save."

"But look at the misery you have created among the people."

"It is the fruit of which they themselves have sown the seed."

"Is there no means of staying this plague?"

"None! I have no more of the elixir. The dervish only gave me one phial, and that I handed to you. In due time the hand of the Lord will save the remnant that survive. To-day and to-morrow are in the hands of God. Blessed be the name of the Lord."

"Oh, Frank," cried Eva, who was kneeling beside the bedside of Sir Luke, "he is dying—save him! save my father!"

"He is not your father," said Malister, walking across the room to the kneeling girl.

"Not my father! What do you mean?"

"I mean that one of you two girls is my daughter, stolen from me by that villain who is dying there."

"Respect the dying," cried Frank, in a tone of entreaty.

"Respect him! Respect the man who robbed me of my wife and child," said Malister, in a tone of scorn. "Let him make restitution for all he has taken away. Let him give me back my years of happiness—my wife, true and faithful—my daughter, and then I will respect him."

"This man is mad," said Laura, in a cold tone, moving tall and stately between the destroyer and his victim; "let him leave this room."

"Mad! yes, I am mad with misery!" retorted Malister, still keeping his position; "but do not speak to me like this. You may be my daughter."

"I am not your daughter."

"Then it is you," said the fanatic, turning to Eva.

"No! no!" she said hurriedly, shrinking back, "this is my father who is dying. Oh, Frank, give him the elixir, and save his life!"

"The elixir!" repeated Malister, recoiling, with a sudden frown on his wrinkled face.

"Yes; you forgot that!" said Frank, producing the phial from his pocket. "See, this is what will save your victim at the eleventh hour."

"So be it," answered the fanatic, in a similar tone. "If it be the will of the Lord that he should live, he shall live; but let him tell me the name of my daughter."

No one made any reply to this demand, and Frank busied himself with preparing the elixir. Having dropped one drop, which was all that he could spare, into a glass of water, he was alarmed to see that the liquid did not change to its usual red colour.

"Three drops! three drops!" said Malister quickly, upon which Rebelspear looked at him incredulously.

"I thought you wanted him to die."

"I want him to tell me the name of my daughter," replied the fanatic, evasively; "but he cannot speak—revive him with that cure, and he will do so. If he lives I say nothing—if he dies I say nothing—to-day and to-morrow are in the hands of God."

Rebelspear looked at Eva, and hesitated whether to use any more of the precious liquid, but the look of agony on her face decided him, and he dropped two more drops into the glass. The water changed to a pale red, but nothing like the deep colour as in his former experiment, which somewhat perplexed him. Still, nothing more could be done, so he hastily held the glass to the dry lips of the baronet and drew back to watch the effect.

Laura, Eva, and Rebelspear were all standing close round the bed, but Malister thrust them fiercely back and bent over his enemy.

"Tell me the name of my daughter—quick—quick!"

Sir Luke opened his eyes, which had closed for a moment, and his sallow cheeks became tinged with red, then with a cry of anguish he raised his head and looked wildly around.

" Eva ! Eva ! "

Malister turned towards the fair-haired girl with a cry of joy, but at this moment Kernshaw fell back on his pillow—dead.

The elixir had failed in its effect. On seeing which, the fanatic appeared transfixed with astonishment.

" Dead ! " he muttered in horror, bending over the still form of his enemy. " Dead !—the elixir ! Why—what does it mean ? "

" I know no more than you," replied Frank, who had turned pale with fear. " It cured once, but this time—well, you can see for yourself."

Malister flung up his hands with a cry of anger,—

" That cursed dervish, he has deceived me."

CHAPTER XII.

REBELSPEAR returned home in a state of great perplexity, being much in doubt as to his future movements. He could do nothing at present with Eva, as she steadfastly refused to leave the body of the dead man until it received decent burial; and as Laura was there to keep her company, Frank came back to his house in order to consult Delicker. The fanatic, filled with joy at having discovered his daughter, also remained in the house of death, although Frank tried to get him away.

"No," he said, fiercely, resisting the entreaties of the young doctor, "the jewel that was lost is found again. Heaven has given me my reward for carrying out my mission, and I lose not sight of my reward."

So in grim silence remained Matthew Malister in the house of his enemy, gloating over his newly-found child; and Frank ran back to Weymouth Street in the hope that Delicker had returned from his self-imposed mission of seeking Malister. The consulting-room was empty, however, when he arrived; and on asking the servant, he learned that Julian was still absent, so he sat wearily down at his desk heart-sick with anxiety and dread.

The afternoon was oppressively hot—so hot, indeed, that London seemed to be one vast furnace; but on the verge of the western horizon loomed a mighty black cloud, above which blazed the sun in intolerable brilliancy. If only the rain would come and drench the pestilent-stricken air for many days, the plague might abate; but while this terrible burning heat continued, the germs of the sickness multiplied with alarming rapidity, and every breath drawn by humanity sucked in the deadly poison. A gentle wind was blowing westward through the plague-cursed city, and seated in his consulting-room Rebelspear could hear the feeble cries of the dying, and the riotous songs of those who tried to forget their terrors in revelry.

He felt dull and depressed, then a shivering fit seized him, and he shook as if he had the ague, but pressing his hands to his burning brow he gazed at the phial he held in his hands, wondering why it had failed to cure Sir Luke. It was most unaccountable this failure, as certainly the same dose had snatched Delicker back from the jaws of death, and then the difference in the crimson colour puzzled him. When he had given it to Delicker the tint was a deep ruby, but when he held it to the fevered lips of Sir Luke, the water was of a pale-looking hue—most strange and inexplicable.

The bells of the church near him began to ring in a mournful fashion, which irritated him extremely, although the reflection that every stroke heralded the last gasp of some unhappy wretch, ought to have inclined him to gentler and more melancholy thoughts. But he felt strangely irritable and perplexed—irritated by the absence of Delicker, and perplexed by the thought of Eva turning out to be Malister's daughter.

Again the shivering fit came on, and this time he was seized with a hideous dread that he had fallen a victim to the plague. With a cry of alarm he arose from his seat, feeling curiously weak, and staggered rather than walked across the room to the mirror hanging over the fireplace. One glance told him all—his face was deeply red—his eyes were dull and heavy—his lips dry and cracked—he was seized with the Burning Sickness.

With a shriek of horror, he touched the ivory button of the electric bell, and as its shrill summons rung through the house, he felt his limbs giving way under him, and in another moment he was lying on the floor without the power to move hand or foot. In answer to the bell his servant ran hastily into the room and recoiled in terror when he saw his master lying motionless on the floor.

"Oh, sir, is it—is it—"

"The plague!" gasped Rebelspear, "the plague."

Selfish thoughts for his own safety overcame all feelings of humanity in the breast of the man, and he turned quickly to leave, when Rebelspear gave such a cry of anguish that he involuntarily stayed.

"Don't go! don't go!—you can cure me."

"Cure you, sir? Impossible!"

"See on the table that phial—pour three drops into a glass of water—it will save my life."

With a bound the man was at the desk and seized the phial, but not to obey his master. No! He placed the phial in his pocket in order to secure his own safety in case of seizure, and fled from the room, pursued by the curses of the man he had deserted so basely.

" Oh, villain, villain ! " moaned Rebelspear in agony, " to leave me thus—Eva ! Eva ! She will be lost, and I—I shall die here like a dog, with no one to aid me. Eva ! Julian ! Malister, help me !—help ! "

It was useless crying like this, as he well knew ; for, no one having the elixir, no one could help him ; but he wanted some human being near him to soothe his dying moments, and therefore called vainly on the woman he loved.

" Eva ! Eva ! I am dying !—Eva ! "

He heard the door open slowly, but owing to his position could see nothing. All his limbs were quite paralysed, and his body was burning with heat, so that he lay immovably on the floor listening in an agony of expectation to the entrance of the newcomer. The rustle of a dress caught his ear, and he uttered a cry of joy.

" Eva ! "

" It is not Eva."

The woman swept into the middle of the room, and there, tall and stately as ever, with a scornful light in her dark eyes, stood Laura Kernshaw looking down at him as he lay like a dog at her feet.

" Miss Kernshaw ! "

" Yes, Laura Kerushaw, who has come to bring you life —or death."

" What do you mean ? "

" I mean that I can save you on conditions."

" Save me ! Impossible ! The elixir is gone ! "

" The elixir is not gone ! " she replied, coldly, drawing a small bottle from her pocket; " it is here ! "

" You have taken it from Philips," he cried, joyfully; " he stole it from me ! "

" No, I have not taken it from Philips ! He may have stolen the phial, as you say, but he did not steal the elixir."

" I—I don't understand," he groaned in agony, rolling his head from side to side on the carpet; " I don't understand ! "

" Listen, then, Frank Rebelspear, lying there smitten by the plague, nor set yourself again against the wit of a woman. When you left this room to-day with my sister, I saw the phial lying on the table—you had told me of its virtues—so wishing to try them, I got a bottle from yonder cabinet and poured the contents of the phial into it. Then I replaced the true elixir with pure water and left it in its old position. You returned and took it, but you carried away only pure water, so now you know the reason you could not cure Sir Luke Kernshaw."

This, then, was the reason that the water had only become tinged with a pale red when he used the elixir for Sir Luke. The pure water put into the original phial by Laura had become impregnated with the thin film of the powerful liquid which still clung to the sides of the bottle, but, being thus weakened, had not been able to act with its full virtue. As this explanation flashed across his mind, he gave a cry of despair.

" Wretch ! demon ! your own father."

" He is not my father ! "

" He is ! Eva is Malister's daughter."

" So he thinks, but it is not so. When Sir Luke died his last cry was for his daughter Eva, and as it came apparently in answer to Malister's question, he thought it was the truth. I am Matthew Malister's daughter, and I have known it for many years, so you see I was not so criminal as you suppose in letting Sir Luke die."

" Ungrateful ! when he was so good to you."

" Good to me," she repeated, in supreme scorn. " Yes ; he ruined my mother—he betrayed my father, and thought to expiate his sin by bringing me up as his own child. Fool that he was ! I was appointed to revenge the past, and I did so by letting him die when I could have saved him."

" God ! are you human ? "

" In my love for you, yes."

" What do you mean ? I am dying ! the plague has seized me, and yet you talk of your love ! Oh, I am suffering the tortures of hell. I burn ! I burn ! "

" Aye, and you shall burn until you say you love me."

" Never ! never ! Love you—a woman who has let her adopted father die."

" Say, rather, who has avenged her mother. This is no time for fine speeches, Dr. Rebelspear. You are lying there in the grip of death ! You cannot live more than twelve hours, and you will pass those twelve hours in agony. From that agony, from that death, I can save you."

" And you will—you will ! " he said, imploringly, turning his eloquently pathetic eyes upon her cold face.

For answer she flung herself on her knees beside him and took his aching head tenderly on her lap.

"My best beloved," she said, in a sweet slow voice, "I will save you to be rich and honoured and happy—with me."

"With you?"

"Yes! Do you not see how I love you—how I worship you? Frank, since I first saw you I have loved you. You are more to me than my good name—than my life—than my soul. Oh, Frank, my darling, say you will be my husband, and I will take you out of this hell wherein you are lying."

. Her tears fell fast from her now tender eyes and rained down on his burning cheeks, but with a great effort he jerked his head off her lap with a cry of rage and scorn.

"Marry you! be your husband! devil that you are, rather will I lie here until I die."

"Frank!"

"A woman who could act as you have done—who could let her adopted father die! O God! the horror of it. Kernshaw betrayed your mother, but he was just to you—he ruined your father, but he was just to you. By false-hood and treachery you have stolen that which would have saved him, and now—now you come to me and ask me to be your husband."

"Frank! Frank! do not be so cruel. See, I that have knelt to no one—not even to Heaven—am kneeling by your side. Promise that you will be my husband and I will give you this elixir! I will save your life, and together we will leave this fated city."

" No ! no ! no !"

" As you are a man, listen !. I have money—plenty of money. It is true I am the daughter of Matthew Malister, but it is also true that I am the co-heiress with Eva of Luke Kernshaw. Let me save you and we will take this money, and go."

" Go ! go ! but alone."

" You will not let me help you ?"

" Not at the price you ask."

She sprang to her feet with tears of rage in her eyes.

" Am I so old and ugly that I am loathsome in your sight ? I am as beautiful as Eva !"

" I love Eva."

" And you do not love me ?"

" No !"

" Beware ! Frank Rebelspear," she said, in a tone of menace, " your life is in my hands."

" My life is in the hands of God."

" Call upon God and see whether He will save you."

" If it is by His will He will save me—even from you."

" I give you one last chance. I have abused my pride for you. I have overstepped the bounds of a woman's modesty in my strong love for a man who does not deserve to have it !"

" I do not desire it ! I love Eva !"

" You will not love me, nor will you love Eva. Oh,

poor thing that you are, to cast away the chance of life for a fancy."

"Go, go!" he moaned, piteously, "leave me to die in peace."

"I will not! See!"

She placed the little bottle close to his lips as he lay on the floor, and laughed tauntingly.

"There is your life; it is yours on the condition I have mentioned."

"Fiend that you are to torture me so; I will not yield— I will not yield! If I die, I die; but never will I be your husband."

"Think of your coming agonies."

"I can bear them—for Eva's sake."

"Eva! Eva! always Eva! I tell you Eva is lost to you! She has the plague."

"It's a lie."

"It's the truth! After you left to-day she was seized, and my father is kneeling beside her, thinking she is his daughter. She is lost! I still live. Take life from my hands and I will spare you."

"Never. If I lose Eva, I lose all. If I lose my life, I lose all—your words confirm my determination. She will die with me, and we will meet in another world far beyond the reach of your malice."

"You will not be my husband?".

"No! no! a thousand times, no!"

"Then die."

She walked proudly to the door, leaving him lying in agony on the floor, and paused a moment on the threshold.

"I give you one more chance."

"Torture me not. I refuse !"

"Coward ! traitor ! then die in your folly. Eva will never be yours, and you will both be buried in a dishonoured grave."

"Happier fate than being with you."

She paused a moment irresolutely on the threshold, then bursting into a peal of mocking laughter, fled, leaving the man, now about to die, alone.

CHAPTER XIII.

BETWEEN LIFE AND DEATH.

THE hot afternoon wore slowly away, and still Frank Rebelspear, alone in his misery, lay on the floor of his consulting-room burning with the fever of the pestilence. Never did time seem to pass so slowly, and every second, ticked out by the clock on the mantelpiece, seemed like an eternity to this hapless human being, helpless in the deadly grip of the plague. Neither hand nor foot could he move, not a limb could he stir, and at last he was unable to move his head, so there he lay, powerless to aid himself, and powerless to call others to his aid.

Would Delicker never return? He had now been out nearly all day searching for Malister, and surely he must have given up the quest long ago, or else—horrible thought! —he had again been seized by the Burning Sickness, and was perhaps lying in agony in the ghastly graveyard of the streets. But no, it was impossible! the plague would not seize him again. He would return shortly—return to save his unhappy friend from death.

No, that could not be! no one could save him except

Laura Kernshaw, and she had vanished for ever, taking with her the precious draught which would have given him life. Eva also was dying and he could not save her. Fool that he was to reveal the virtues of the elixir and trust to the honour of humanity in this crisis of the world's history. He had unwittingly deceived his servant that the original phial contained the elixir, and the servant had treacherously fled with it. He had seen the real cure in the hand of Laura Kernshaw, and because he refused to accept her love and surrender Eva she had left him to perish in torments worse than those of the Inquisition. Oh, it was terrible to die like this—alone! unfriended! with no one to give him a drop of water to quench his burning thirst; no one to close his eyes when he died. He must die! he must die, and then—

But no! Hope, the good fairy, who had fled from the Weymouth Street house on the fatal night when Malister first revealed his terrible mission, now returned to comfort the unhappy man. It was true that the elixir was gone, but in yonder cabinet was the glass containing the draught which he had prepared in order to see the nature of the cure. He had placed it there and forgotten all about it. Now he was safe if he could only reach the cabinet and drink the life-giving liquid. But how was he to reach the cabinet? He was powerless to move, and lying on the floor, only a few steps separated him from life; yet these few steps he was unable to take. It was terrible thus to perish,

so to speak, within sight of land. Yonder was the cabinet
containing the already prepared draught, and here he lay, a
helpless log, unable to help himself in any way whatsoever.
His brain was clear, but his limbs were paralysed, and he
felt as if he were in one of those horrible trances which
entail burial alive.

If he could only call aid; but that was impossible; the
disease had now seized his throat, and already his voice was
hoarse and broken. Besides, if he did call out it would be
no use. The servants had all fled from the plague-stricken
house, and he was left to die alone! Die! no, he would
not die! his life was in that cabinet, but it was as far away
from him in his helplessness as if separated by leagues of
roaring sea.

With a violent effort he tried to shriek, but only a hoarse,
broken murmur issued from his lips, which could hardly be
heard, so all he could do was to lie there speechless, motionless, consumed as with fire, and with his eyes fixed in despair
on the mahogany cabinet near the writing-table, the cabinet
which contained his life.

The wind was rising, and he could hear it blowing shrilly
through the windows and round the house. Its cold breath,
laden with moisture, touched his burning forehead like a
gentle hand, and he saw that the sunlight was dying away,
while the blue spot of sky, seen through the window, became
black with clouds. A change had taken place in the weather
—the intense heat of the past two months was at an end;

and now there came a cold wind—soon there would come the rain, and perchance the plague would be swept away from the ill-fated city. But of what use was it to him—he was dying—he would die, and no one could save him from his fate.

" Julian ! "

With preternaturally sharp hearing he caught the sound of Delicker's light steps bounding up the stairs, and in another moment his friend was in the room. For the space of a minute he stood looking at the still figure lying on the floor ; and then with a cry of bitter anguish he sprang forward and flung himself on his knees beside his dying friend.

" Frank ! Frank ! Has the plague seized you at last ? Oh, my poor fellow ; where is the elixir you cured me with ? Quick ! quick ! I will give it to you at once. "

Rebelspear could make no answer, owing to the paralysis of his throat, and could only look at the anxious face of the young man with a look of dumb agony.

" Can you not speak ? " cried Delicker, in despair. " Great heavens ! you must have been hours like this. All the servants are gone, I suppose. If I could only find that phial."

Delicker wrung his hands in despair, for he did not know where to look for the phial which he supposed was still in Frank's possession, and Frank could not tell him in any way, neither by writing nor by speaking, seeing that the paralysis of the disease had rendered useless both his throat and hands. With the hope of despair Julian sprang to his feet and began to search about the room, looking everywhere except—by some strange chance—in the cabinet. Frank saw him searching—knew where the cure was, yet was compelled to lie there speechless and immovable, without having the power to direct his friend where to look.

"My God!" cried Julian, in despair, looking at the still figure, "what am I to do?"

He searched again and again, even opened the cabinet; but as he was hunting for the phial he naturally looked for it and quite passed over the glass of red water standing on the lower shelf. Rebelspear saw him leave the cabinet with a feeling of despair and gave himself up for lost. Julian, desisting from his useless search, flung himself on his knees by his friend, and looked steadily at the sick man's eyes. A sudden idea had struck him of applying the system in Dumas' novel, "Monte Christo," by which Noirtier, the old paralytic, is made to express his meaning by raising and lowering his eyelids.

"Frank," said Julian, "do you remember Noirtier in 'Monte Christo,' how he made known his wishes by his eyes? If you can use your eyelids, answer me in the same way. Close your eyes for 'yes' and leave them open for 'no.' Do you understand?"

Frank closed his eyes, upon which Julian gave a cry of

joy, and began to interpret rapidly according to the "yes" or "no" of the eyes.

"Good! the paralysis has not yet affected your eyelids. Now, tell me—is the phial in your pocket? No. Is it in the desk? No. Is it in the room? No. Why!" cried Julian, in surprise, "what does this mean? Not in the room! have you lost it?"

Frank closed his eyes again, to signify yes, and Julian sprang to his feet in dismay.

"Lost!" he said in alarm. "Great heavens! then you cannot be saved?"

The sick man closed his eyes once more.

"What! have you another phial? No! Well then, you cannot be cured! Yes. You say yes. Why, what does he mean?" muttered Julian in perplexity, looking round the room. "If the phial is lost, I certainly can't save him."

He looked again at the sick man, but saw that his eyes were looking past him, upon which he suddenly turned round to see upon what the gaze was fixed.

"The desk? No. The window? No. The cabinet? Yes. Ah, there is something in the cabinet; but I looked there, and found nothing."

He rapidly began to take the medicine bottles out of the cabinet.

"This? No. This? No. This? No. Why, Frank, there are no more bottles. Is it a bottle? No. Then,

what is it? A powder? No. A draught? Yes. In a
glass? Yes. Ah!" cried Julian in a tone of joy, "is this
it?" and he held out the glass filled with the red liquid to
Frank.

"Yes," said the eyes in the most eloquent manner; and
with a cry of delight Julian knelt down beside his friend and
held the draught to his lips. Rebelspear drained it to
the last drop, and then fell into a deep sleep, upon seeing which Julian lifted him in his arms and placed him
gently on the sofa, then sat down beside him, in order to
watch.

The darkness fell at last over the hot, dry earth, but
now the cool gloom was damp with moisture, and the wind
was blowing boisterously. As Julian sat by the sofa in the
darkness, he could hear the fierce blasts rushing madly
down the street, and on going to the window he saw that
the sky was filled with flying clouds, rushing across the
pale moon, the bright stars, and the fierce blaze of the
comet. The long street was quite deserted; the gas
lamps were not lighted, nor was there any sound of
traffic or of human voices. It was truly terrible—this
silence in the mighty city, and the wailing wind
sweeping down the empty streets seemed to lament
for the dead who had been slain by the sword of the
pestilence.

The comet seemed paler than before, so, without doubt,
it was receding from the earth, and Julian put up a prayer

—yes, this scoffer and unbeliever put up a prayer—that with the comet might pass the scourge of the Burning Sickness. Formerly he had not believed in the existence of a God; but, since his escape from death, his thoughts had taken a new turn, and he was sceptical no longer; and here, in the midst of the terrible desolation of London, he knelt by the window with a prayer on his lips that God would not utterly destroy the metropolis of the world.

Frank was breathing regularly and gently, which Julian judged to be a good sign, and on placing his hand upon the sick man's forehead he found it covered with a profuse perspiration, so he felt sure that the elixir had done its work, and the Burning Sickness had left his friend.

With waiting, watching, and anxiety, he was quite worn out, so he took a glass of wine and some biscuits, after which he felt better, then returning to his post by the sofa, he remained watching all the night by Rebelspear's side. The heavy hours rolled slowly by, the gloom deepened, the gloom lightened, and, lo ! in the sombre sky burned the crimson splendours of the dawn. The wind, still increasing, was now blowing a gale, and every blast seemed to shake the house, while Julian could hear the falling of tiles and chimney-pots, wrenched off by the force of the hurricane.

One fierce burst shook the house to its foundations, then for a moment there was a dead stillness, in the midst of which Frank awoke, and smiled gratefully on the man who had saved him.

"I am cured of the plague," he said, quietly; "give me some wine, Julian, and I will tell you all I have suffered."

CHAPTER XIV.

FOUND AND LOST.

"Good heavens!" cried Julian, when Frank had related to him the strange experiences of the previous day, "what a fiend of a woman! I certainly don't envy Malister his newly-found daughter."

"But you forget, Malister looks upon Eva as his daughter."

"True! Now, of course, you will undeceive him, Frank?"

Rebelspear walked thoughtfully across to the window, and looked out at the lonely street. A little way along lay the body of some poor wretch who, having been seized with the Burning Sickness, had fallen to the ground and died where he had fallen. Above, a dull, grey sky; below, the dull, grey earth; and lying there in that dreary solitude, the lonely corpse, with its ghastly face turned appealingly to the sombre heavens. It was truly a terrible scene, and one which Rebelspear in after years never forgot. He was not thinking of the scene at present, however, but meditating over the question Julian had put to him.

"No," he said at last, in a low voice. "I don't think I will undeceive him."

"And why not?"

"Malister thinks Eva is his daughter, and Laura says Eva has been seized by the plague, so, in that case, her supposed father will do all he can to save her."

"But how can he save her?"

"By giving her the elixir, of course."

"You forget Laura has the elixir."

"Of course; but I hardly think Malister would have parted entirely with his only hope of safety. No; you may be sure, Julian, that he has more of that elixir; and if—as Laura said—Eva has been seized with the plague, he will cure her."

"I don't believe what Laura says," said Julian, impetuously; "very likely she told you Eva was stricken only to cause you more pain in thinking you could not aid her. However, as—according to Laura—twelve hours have passed since Eva was seized, she must, if that is true, be dead by this time."

"I am sure Malister will save her," said Frank, hopefully; "but if I were to tell him that Laura is his daughter, he would take no trouble with Eva, particularly as she is the child of his bitterest enemy; so I will keep silence. And you too, Julian, say nothing."

" Oh, I will not open my mouth ; but I think the best thing we can do is to go at once and see after Eva."

" First, however, we must have breakfast. I feel faint for want of food."

" You are not a very ardent lover, Frank," said Julian, in a tone of faint reproach.

" I can do no good," replied Frank, drearily. " God knows I love Eva dearer than my own life ; but Laura has robbed me of the means of saving her. If she is seized by the plague she must die—unless, indeed, Malister saves her, as he will certainly do."

" Provided he has another phial of the elixir," said Delicker, significantly.

Frank nodded languidly, and they went down to the kitchen in order to search for some food. The terrible experience through which he had passed had quite worn out the young doctor, and he moved about in a listless, weary fashion, which caused Julian serious uneasiness.

" Good Lord ! Frank, do try to pull yourself together," he said, when they were seated at a hastily provided meal ; " you seem to have lost all interest in life."

" I feel worn out after last night, Julian ; but when I have had some food I shall be all right."

" Frank, my poor fellow, you are fretting about Eva."

" True, I feel that I cannot help her if she is plague-stricken."

" I tell you I don't believe that. It is a fiendish device

of that woman's to torture you. Look here, my boy, you doctors don't know how to treat yourselves. Come upstairs now we have finished, and have a good glass of wine to revive you."

Rebelspear agreed to this and they slowly returned to the consulting-room. When approaching it they heard a low, wailing cry which froze the blood in their veins.

"Why, what is that?" gasped Julian, standing suddenly still.

"Eva, Eva!" cried Rebelspear, his thoughts at once reverting to the woman he loved, and without another word he hastily mounted the remaining steps and dashed into the consulting-room.

"Malister!"

It was indeed Malister, who stood there looking more shadowy than ever, with a wild look on his face, as the wind fluttered his loose black garments. On seeing Frank he sprang forward with another cry, but this time one of joy, and laid his claw-like hands on the arm of the astonished young man.

"Where is it? where is it?"

"What?"

"The cure! the phial! I want it for my daughter, for Eva."

"Is she dead?" shrieked Rebelspear, in despair.

"Dead! No! But she soon will be. She was seized with the plague this morning."

" Not last night ? "

" No ; she has only been ill an hour."

" Thank Heaven ! " cried Julian, with a sigh of relief; "there is still time; but why don't you cure her, Malister?"

" I ? " wailed the fanatic. " I would cure her if I could, but I cannot."

" You have not another phial of the elixir ? " said Frank, his face growing grey with anguish.

" No, no ! I gave you all I had. Heaven help me; I never thought for a moment that I should require it. Having punished this generation by the plague, I was content to die, but now that I have found my dear daughter I want to save her. Oh, you say that you love her—if so, give me that phial and I will bring her back again to life."

" I cannot give you the elixir."

" Man ! man ! have you no heart ? " cried Malister, throwing himself on the floor and clutching Rebelspear's knees ; " I tell you my daughter—my child who was lost and is now found—is dying. That elixir can save her. It failed with Kershaw, but it may succeed with my child. Give it to me at once. I helped you, now I call upon you to help me."

" I cannot."

" Wretch ! "

" Spare your reproaches," said Rebelspear, withdrawing himself from the grip of the fanatic. " I would save Eva if I could, not for your sake, but for my own, but I cannot. The elixir is not in my possession.

B

Malister jumped up with a frightful cry, and plucked at his long white beard as if he would wrench it out by the roots.

" You have lost it ? "

" No ; it was stolen from me."

"Stolen ! and by whom ? ".

" Miss Laura Kernshaw.".

The old man looked at Rebelspear in surprise, and for a moment there was silence ; after which, Julian, seeing that his friend was too overcome by emotion to speak, hastened to explain.

' "Laura Kernshaw is in love with Dr. Rebelspear," he said, slowly, " and stole the elixir from this room in order to force him to return her affection. She had it in her possession when Sir Luke was dying, and saw Rebelspear give him the water she substituted for the real cure, without trying to save the old man's life."

" Her own father," cried Malister, bitterly. " Oh, worthy daughter of such a father."

There was something painfully grotesque in this speech, as both the young men knew that, inadvertently, Malister spoke of himself.

"Laura Kernshaw," pursued Julian, smoothly, "came here yesterday, and found Rebelspear plague-stricken. She offered him the elixir if he would marry her, but he refused, so she left him to die."

" To die ! " echoed the fanatic, in surprise ; " but you did not die • "

"No," answered Rebelspear, hastily; "luckily I had tried the effect of the elixir shortly after you gave it to me and put the preparation I had made away in yonder cabinet, where it was forgotten. My friend here found it, and I was saved."

" Then Laura Kernshaw has the real elixir?"

"Yes."

"But she is with Eva," stammered the old man in perplexity; "I left her with Eva. She can cure her if she will."

"Yes, but she will not," said Julian, seeing that Frank remained silent. "She loves Rebelspear, and wants your daughter to die, so that he may love her."

"Oh, just God!" cried Malister, lifting his hands to Heaven; "how hast Thou punished me for mine iniquity! I believed I was doing Thy will in blotting out London from the cities of the earth; but lo! I acted but as my folly swayed me, and now the weapon that I forged for others is turned against me."

" You must save your daughter," said Julian, decisively.

" But how? in what way?"

"Let us all go to Park Lane and insist upon Laura Kernshaw giving up the elixir."

"Yes, yes," cried Malister, putting on his hat; "we will go at once. I will force her to give up that which she has stolen, even if I have to kill her to do so."

" Kill her?" cried the young men, struck with horror.

"Yes. Do you think that I value my life in comparison with that of my child? Let the daughter of Luke Kernshaw perish—let me perish myself—let all London perish, but my child must be saved. Come! come, young men, let us go quickly lest she dies in the arms of that traitoress."

"I was right, you see," whispered Frank, as the old man glided out of the room and they followed; "if I had told him the truth he would not have saved Eva."

"Laura will tell him the truth when she finds out that he wants to kill her."

"Let her," retorted Frank, firmly, "as long as I get the elixir from her and save my darling."

By this time they were in the street, and could see Malister far in front of them, being blown along like a gigantic leaf. Indeed, so terrible was the force of the wind, that they found it difficult themselves to maintain their equilibrium, and their pace being accelerated by the fierce blasts, they fled, rather than walked, towards Park Lane. The street was strewn with broken chimney-pots, tiles, glass, and other vestiges of the wind's work during the night, but there was no sign of it failing, and it howled through London under the bleak grey sky as if it were searching for the plague to draw it forth from the city it had cursed.

"I'm glad of this wind," shrieked Frank in the ears of Julian as they staggered along.

" Why ? "

"It will stay the plague. It will blow all the germs away, and if the rain comes afterwards it will sweep the city clean."

Julian made no reply, as the roaring of the tempest was so loud that he could not make himself heard, and, indeed, he had missed the gist of Frank's speech, so they raced onward after that shadowy black form which glided ahead like an ill-omened bird of prey.

CHAPTER XV.

THE SINS OF THE FATHER.

WHO was that lying upon the white bed so still and silent, with her hands crossed on her breast and her terror-filled eyes staring at the ceiling? Was it Eva Kernshaw or her statue, the living woman or her dead body? In truth, it could have been taken for the dead, save for the anguish in the wide open eyes. The plague had seized her only an hour before, and already her limbs were paralysed so that she could make no movement, but she could still speak in a low whisper. When the disease arrived at her throat, however, that also would be taken away and she would be dead indeed—dead in all respects save as to the separation of the soul from the body.

The room was in disorder, clothes hastily thrown about, the window blinds askew, dust everywhere, and no sound but the steady ticking of the clock, measuring out the grains of time that still remained to her of this earthly life. She was alone, no one was beside her, and the unhappy girl felt all the agony of soul endured by her lover before her.

Malister, who said he was her father, had left her, the servants had all fled, Laura was in another part of the house, and she was lying on the disordered bed waiting the sure approach of death.

"Frank! Frank!" she cried, in a tone of agony, "oh, where are you, Frank? Can you not save me from this?"

No answer, but suddenly outside in the garden sounded the song of a bird which pierced shrilly through the tumult of the wind. The rich notes comforted her for a moment and then seemed to wring her heart with pain, as they brought to mind all she had lost. Once she was rich in wealth, and health, and love—once she had a father and a lover, but now the father was dead, and the lover had fled where she knew not. Even her sister, Laura, who professed some affection for her, had left her to die alone, and there was not a soul in Heaven or on earth who cared for her in this miserable state.

How the wind howled round the house; it was blowing a perfect hurricane, and she shuddered with inward dread at the thought that her soul released from her body would soon be tossed about on the wings of the fierce blast. If Frank could only save her—but it was impossible. His story of the elixir was false, as it had failed to cure her father. Her father! who was her father?—the dead man who lay in the darkened room below, or this fierce, aged fanatic who had lately left her? She did not know, and in the extremity of her terror at the near approach of death she did not care. All she wanted was Frank, and on Frank she called again and again in a hoarse whisper, only to hear nothing in reply save the fitful song of the bird, and the howling of the wind.

"Oh, Frank! Frank! save me from death!"

This time it was not the wind, but her sister who replied. Her sister, impossible! Could this be her sister, this cruel, cold woman who stood by her death-bed laughing mockingly at her anguish?

"Laura!"

"Yes, it is Laura come to see you die."

"Save me."

"No, I will not save you!"

"Oh, God! my sister—"

"I am not your sister. You are the daughter of Matthew Malister."

"It is not true. You know it is not true!"

"I know many things of which you are ignorant. You say it is not true; you are right. I am the daughter of Matthew Malister. I have known it for years but have never told it to you until now. And why do I tell you now? Because you are dying and cannot harm me."

"I have no wish to harm you."

"So you say, Eva," sneered the other woman, with a flash of hatred darting from her eyes; "but what have you done save harm me all my life? I am as beautiful as you, yet all admired you more than me. Frank Rebelspear is the man I love and he gave his heart to you—"

"Oh, Frank! Frank!" wailed the girl, "come and save me."

"He cannot save you. He is dead."

"No! no!"

"It is true I tell you. Yesterday I went to see him and found him lying plague-stricken as you are now. I would have saved his life if he had promised to marry me, but he refused, so I left him to die."

"To marry you—he is mine—mine only."

"So the fool said; but had he been wise he would have given you up, and let me save him."

"Save him! You could not have done so! You have not the power."

"I have the power, my sweet sister; but I have not the will. I could have saved your lover's life. I can save yours. Do you see this phial—it contains the elixir which cures the plague, and I took it from Frank Rebelspear's desk."

"Oh, Laura! give it to me. Let me drink!"

"No, you shall die!"

"Laura!" cried Eva in desperation, "I am so young to die! Oh, do not let me die!"

"I will! I refuse to save your life," replied Laura,

cruelly, putting the phial again in her pocket. "Your lover is dead and you can join him."

Eva gave a cry of anguish as she saw Laura turn away from the bed—a hoarse broken cry, which was the last sound that issued from her throat, for the disease had by this time attacked her vocal chords, and when she tried to cry out again she could not articulate a word. Laura, hearing the curious sound she made, guessed the cause, and returning swiftly to the side of the bed, stood looking down at the unhappy girl with a vengeful smile.

"It comes! it comes! You have lost the use of your limbs. You have lost the use of your voice. Your lover is dead, so you have lost all."

Eva looked at her with a strange reproach in her eyes, the meaning of which Laura guessed at once.

"I know what you would say if you could speak. That I also shall be seized by the plague. Be it so? I can cure myself with this I have in my pocket. I shall escape the pestilence and inherit all the wealth of the man who betrayed my father and ruined my mother, but you will die as your lover has died, and be no more remembered."

She turned away with a scornful smile and went to the door, leaving Eva in a state of agony, both mental and physical, that can be better imagined than described. The clock struck eleven with a silvery chime, and Laura had opened the door in order to leave the room, wherein her rival was dying, when suddenly she heard the sound of hurried footsteps on the stairs, and in another moment was thrust back into the chamber of death by Matthew Malister.

"Where is it, you daughter of sin?" cried the fanatic, seizing her wrist with his bony hand. "Give it to me or I will kill you!"

"What do you mean?"

"The elixir! the elixir. Give it to me."

"I cannot give you what I have not got," said Laura, recovering her firmness with wonderful celerity on recognising her danger. "What elixir are you talking about?"

"The phial you stole from Dr. Rebelspear!"

"I stole nothing! who says I did?"

"Rebelspear himself!"

"He lied if he said so, and you lie in saying he did. I stole nothing from Dr. Rebelspear, and he is dead!"

At this moment Frank, pale as a ghost, appeared on the threshold of the room.

"He is not dead, Laura Kernshaw!"

"Frank!"

She turned white with terror, and reeling against the wall, would have fallen, had not Malister caught her in his arms.

"The elixir! the elixir," he cried, furiously shaking her, "demon that you are, my poor girl is dying. Give me that which will save her."

"I have not got it," gasped Laura, white with terror, "I swear I have not got it."

By this time Frank had crossed the room, and was now kneeling by the side of Eva's bed, but when he heard the last words of Laura, he turned round quickly with a frown.

"That is not true," he said sharply; "you stole the elixir from my room yesterday, so it is now in your possession."

Laura bit her nether lip angrily and looked about for some way of escape. The window, Malister stood before it. The door, Julian Delicker frowned on the threshold. There was certainly no means of escape. They knew she had the elixir and would take it away from her—by force if necessary. Still she would baffle them, for her woman's wit came to her aid, and, sinking into a chair, she burst into tears.

"Oh, Frank, Frank! how can you speak to me like this, when I loved you so?"

"I know what your love is worth; you left me to die."

"I was mad with rage."

"Woman!" cried Malister, his eyes gleaming with mad fire, "this is no time to talk thus. Give me that which you have taken or I—I will strangle you."

"I have not got it with me," she replied, lying with ready subtlety.

" Then where is it ? "

" In my bedroom ; I will go and fetch it ! "

She arose to her feet and stole towards the door, but with such a crafty look on her beautiful face, that Frank called out to Julian to follow her as he did not trust her in any way. Julian, who was also very mistrustful, went after her at once, and although she pretended that she did not notice his movements, she was in reality thinking of how she could rid herself of him, and circumvent those men who had her in their power.

To this end, having hit upon an idea, she went into her room, and was followed closely by Julian. Turning towards him with a look of cold hatred, she pointed to a cabinet at the end of the apartment.

"Since you have forced me to tell my secret, Mr. Delicker, and it is not in my power to protect myself, you will find the elixir in that cabinet."

Julian without a word walked to the end of the room, upon which, with a jeering cry, she darted from the apartment, closed the door and locked it, so that before he could collect his scattered senses, he was a prisoner.

Then rapidly descending the stairs without waiting to put on a cloak or a hat, Laura Kernshaw, in her

fluttering white dress, fled from the house like some
guilty being—fled into the howling tempest, into the
plague-stricken city, whither she neither knew nor
cared.

CHAPTER XVI

MEANWHILE Rebelspear and Malister remained in Eva's room, the former still kneeling beside the bed with his eyes fixed on the flushed face of the sick girl, the latter with folded arms standing near the window muttering prayers. The bird, dismayed by the tempest, had ceased its song, and the fierce wind, increasing every minute, tore furiously round the house under the dull leaden-coloured sky, its shrill complainings mingling curiously with the monotonous ticking of the clock.

As the minutes passed, and Julian did not return, Frank at last became uneasy at his non-appearance. Laura was a very dangerous woman, and in this time of lawless terror when all bonds were loosed by the dread of the pestilence he thought that she would be guilty of any crime in order to secure her own ends. Expecting his friend every minute, however, he said nothing at first, but at the end of a quarter-of-an-hour was about to speak to the fanatic when the door opened and Julian rushed into the room.

137

"Frank, is she here? is she here?"

"Laura?"

"Yes! she decoyed me into a room under the pretence of looking for the elixir, and then locked me up. I managed to escape by the window, and came straight here! Where is she?"

"Great heavens!" cried Frank, rising to his feet, "she must have fled and taken the elixir with her! Poor Eva! now she must die."

"Die," said Malister in his deep-toned voice, "not so! Let us pursue this daughter of Belial and take that which she has stolen, from her."

"But perhaps she has thrown it away."

"Impossible! she will keep it in order to save her own life!"

"Who will go after her?"

"I will," said Malister, moving towards the door; "we will soon find her. She wears a white dress and cannot have fled far in this mighty wind."

"Frank," said Julian, hastily, "Malister is right—the wind is so terrible that she cannot have gone far. You go with him to look for her, and I will wait here by the side of Eva."

Rebelspear assented at once and, accompanied by Malister, went outside into the roaring wind. Park Lane was quite deserted, but it was dangerous to traverse as chimney-pots and tiles were constantly being hurled to the ground by

the force of the tempest. At the gate of the house they
found a poor plague-stricken wretch with just the capability
of speech. There he lay helplessly paralysed, like Lazarus
at the gate of Dives, but Dives himself was in a worse
plight, seeing that he lay dead within.

"Have you seen a woman pass out?" asked Rebelspear,
bending down to this miserable object.

"Water! water!" moaned the man, thickly, "water!"

Anxious to obtain a reply to his question, Frank went
inside and soon returned with a jug of water, which the
poor wretch drained to the bottom. All this time Malister,
with folded arms, stood like a statue of bronze, and never
by word or deed appeared to feel remorse for the frightful
evil he had brought upon the city of which this poor plague-
struck wretch was an example. Frank repeated his question,
and had to place his ear to the sick man's mouth to hear
the reply, so loud was the wind.

"Yes! went down towards Piccadilly!"

"Piccadilly!" echoed Rebelspear, turning to Malister,
but the old man had already started in that direction, and
Frank saw him with bowed head some little distance away
battling with the fierce wind. He followed at once as he
could do no good to the victim of the plague, and with a
great effort caught up to Malister. The fanatic's lips were
moving as in prayer, and as Rebelspear had quite enough
to do in beating up against the fierce blast he said nothing
to his aged companion, and the two men struggled doggedly

F

onward amid the terrors of the tempest. In their path were great boughs of trees torn off by the wind, portions of railings, a smashed-up cabman's shelter, and the Poets' Fountain near Hamilton Place was snapped off its pedestal and lying in ruins some little distance away.

Piccadilly itself represented a very gruesome sight, as in the centre of the road and on the pavements lay many corpses, and slowly lumbering down the road came closed carts in order to collect the dead bodies and take them away for burial. Some specially fierce blast of wind had lifted the roof of one of the houses completely off and hurled it into the roadway, where it lay, a terrible wreck, and under it the bodies of some unhappy wretches it had stricken down. Frank could, however, see no sign of Laura, and asked one of the drivers of the death carts if he had seen a young woman bare-headed and dressed in white. After a moment's reflection the driver said he had seen her turning down St. James Street, but he did not know where she was going.

Considerably pleased at this intelligence, Rebelspear hurried along with his companion as quickly as possible, and speedily found themselves in St. James Street. It now, however, became dangerous to proceed owing to the gale, which was now like a cyclone as it rushed over London, leaving ruin and desolation behind it. Those unhappy beings who, seized by the plague, were unable to fly to shelter, lay directly in the way of all the missles hurled by the furious wind, and at last in Pall Mall Rebelspear had to shrink into a doorway to escape being crushed to death.

Not so Malister, however. The Prophet of Doom moved onward amid the desolation he had created as if he had a charmed life, and anxious not to lose sight of him, Frank at last ventured out of his place of safety and battled along in the direction of Trafalgar Square.

There was no sign of Laura Kernshaw, however, and Frank despaired of ever finding her, when, on emerging into Trafalgar Square, through Cockspur Street, he saw, or thought he saw, a white figure crouching at the base of Nelson's Column. Followed by Malister, he hurried towards this, and found himself face to face with Laura Kernshaw.

"Too late!" she cried in a jeering voice, "too late! I have the plague."

"The plague!" said Malister, with gloomy triumph. "I am glad of it!"

"You?" she said with a bitter smile. "You?"

There was silence for a moment, and the three looked at one another. The square was filled with the dead and the dying, principally crowded round the fountain, whither they had crawled to assuage their thirst, but many of the statues were blown down, crushing in their fall the poor wretches who lay helplessly below. The equestrian statue of Charles the First, however, still stood erect, daring the wind to blow it from its eminence, and round and round the square howled the cyclone furiously, as if it would level everything to the ground.

Luckily, Laura, seized with the plague, had sunk down on the lee side of Nelson's Column, but the great pillar was swaying ominously, and after a hurried glance, Frank bent down to pick up Laura and carry her to a place of safety.

"No! no!" she cried, repulsing him. "Let me die where I have fallen."

"But the column—there is danger."

"I care not! I have the plague! I must die!"

Malister, who had been gloomily surveying the countenance of the fallen woman, now broke out furiously into speech.

"The elixir; the elixir?"

"It is here, in my pocket," she said, coldly; "but I think the phial is broken."

"Ah!" Frank uttered a cry of alarm.

"Yes," said Laura, jeeringly, "you will never marry Eva—she will die, as I die now. I have lost you, but you will never be her husband."

"Give me the phial," cried Malister, furiously.

"No; I will not."

For answer he bent down and thrust his hand into her pocket, while she, paralysed by the Burning Sickness, was unable to prevent him.

"Oh, I hope it is broken; I hope it is broken!" she kept on saying vindictively.

" No, it is not broken," said Frank with a cry of joy, as Malister pulled out the phial from Laura's pocket " Oh, Eva ! Eva will be safe."

He snatched the phial from the old man, and was about to dart off, when a terrible cry from Laura stayed his steps.

" No, no !" she cried, looking at Malister in agony, " give it to me ; give it to me !"

" No; you shall die ! daughter of my enemy, as you are."

" I am not the daughter of your enemy ; I am your daughter !"

He recoiled with a cry of horror.

" Mine ? Impossible !"

" Yes, yes ! I tell you I am. Sir Luke called upon Eva as he died ; and you thought she was your child ; but it is not true. I am ! I am ! Give me the phial—quick ! quick !"

Malister darted forward and seized Frank.

" The phial !—quick !—to save my child !"

" No ; no !" cried Rebelspear, trying to wrench himself away ; " it is for Eva ! Eva !"

" Never !"

Then began a terrible struggle between the two men. Malister, though old, was strong and wiry, so it was doubtful as to who would win the victory, while they twisted, and writhed, and wrestled, and reeled, all the time being encouraged by the voice of the dying woman under the pillar.

"Get it from him, father.　Save me; save your child!"

Malister had his clutch in the throat of Frank, and the young doctor felt his strength giving way under that merciless grip; but he fought on, blindly thinking of what it meant if he lost the battle.

"Eva!"

One cry, and with a Herculean effort, he hurled the old man from him.　Malister tripped, stumbled, and fell beside his daughter, while Frank, with the precious phial in his pocket, fled as if pursued by a thousand demons.

A furious blast of wind caught him at the end of the square and dashed him ou the ground, from whence he looked up, to see the mighty Column reel, totter, and fall, with a crash like thunder.

And under it—divided in life, but together in death—lay the bodies of Matthew Malister and his newly-found child.

CHAPTER XVII.

NEW ENGLAND.

THAT terrible storm which swept over London was a blessing in disguise, for although it devastated and laid in ruins a great part of the mighty city, yet it swept the streets clean of the plague. After the wind came the rain which fell in sheets as if the windows of heaven were again open, as in the days of Noah. For days did that mighty rain drench the city, and when again the sky was blue and the winds had ceased, all trace of the Burning Sickness had passed away from London.

Nor indeed was this good work of the storm confined to London alone, for far and wide through the length and breadth of the United Kingdom it swept, cleansing with terrible force the plague-stricken cities, until at last the pestilence utterly departed from Great Britain and Ireland.

Order was once more restored in London, the dead were all buried, the houses cleansed and purified, and life began again; but not the old life, for this frightful visitation of the

Burning Sickness marked the beginning of a new epoch in England. With the dawn of the twentieth century dawned a new life better than the old.

The hundreds and thousands that had perished in the great pestilence had left more room for those who survived, and the consequence was that work and food became plentiful. A great number of the poorer classes had been swept away, and in this case of the survival of the fittest those left in England to rebuild London, and the social life of the British people, were mostly either physically or mentally strong. The brain workers aided the physically strong in the work of rebuilding a new England out of the ruins of the old, and the twentieth century began its career under the happiest auspices.

One of the foremost workers of the new age was Dr. Rebelspear, who married Eva Kernshaw very shortly after the plague had ceased. The elixir did its work and she was saved to become Frank's wife and to make his life happy after all the terrors through which he had passed. Julian Delicker acted as best man, and although the wedding was a very quiet one, seeing that the terror of the Burning Sickness had not yet passed away, yet it was very happy, and many a time afterwards did Frank congratulate himself upon having saved Eva from the pestilence and thus gained such a charming wife.

Julian Delicker, too, was changed. No longer the gay society butterfly he had been in former years, he devoted

his days and wealth to the rebuilding of the new system
and to doing good to his fellow-creatures. The idle words
he had spoken in jest about a plague had been realised in
deadly earnest, and although there was no doubt that in
the end the plague proved to have been a boon, seeing that
it had swept away the surplus population, yet the whole
affair was too terrible for any one to wish it to be repeated.

Whether Malister had actually brought the germs of the
plague from the East, or whether the story of the city of
Nar was a fable, Rébelspear could never clearly make out,
but one thing was certain, that those deadly germs had
multiplied very rapidly in the burning air of those months
of June and July, so that he was entirely responsible for the
frightful catastrophe which had befallen London. The
bodies of the old fanatic and his daughter were found
crushed to death under the ruins of Nelson's Column, and
Rebelspear buried them both in one grave, while the body
of Sir Luke was placed in a grave not far from that of his
old enemy.

Taking an example from the errors of the past, the
Government of England formulated a scheme by which they
hoped to do away entirely with a pauper population. The
plague had cleansed as with fire the slums of Whitechapel
and the low parts of London of their criminal population,
and seeing that only the strong and healthy were left, these
were made to work. Idleness was not permitted to either
man or woman; marriage between those weakly, either

mentally or physically, was forbidden, and altogether the rulers of the people did all in their power to aid the development of the English race so as to abolish from their midst disease, crime, and poverty.

The great comet which had burned so near to the earth passed entirely away, and with it passed the Burning Sick-ness. The nineteenth century with its overcrowded England, its crimes and its follies, also passed away, and in its place dawned the twentieth century full of promise and hope to humanity.

Long afterwards, when things under the new system were going smoothly, Frank was talking to Julian of that terrible time.

"Ah !" he said, at length, when they had discussed the subject for some time, " it was a frightful year, but still a year from which all that is good in this present century will spring."

"' Out of the mouth of the spoiler came forth sweet-ness,'" quoth Julian, eagerly; " the plague was most miraculous."

" Well, then," said Rebelspear, gaily, " we will steal an idea from Tennyson, and call nineteen hundred the Year of Miracle."

THE END.

Cowan & Co., Limited, Printers, Perth.

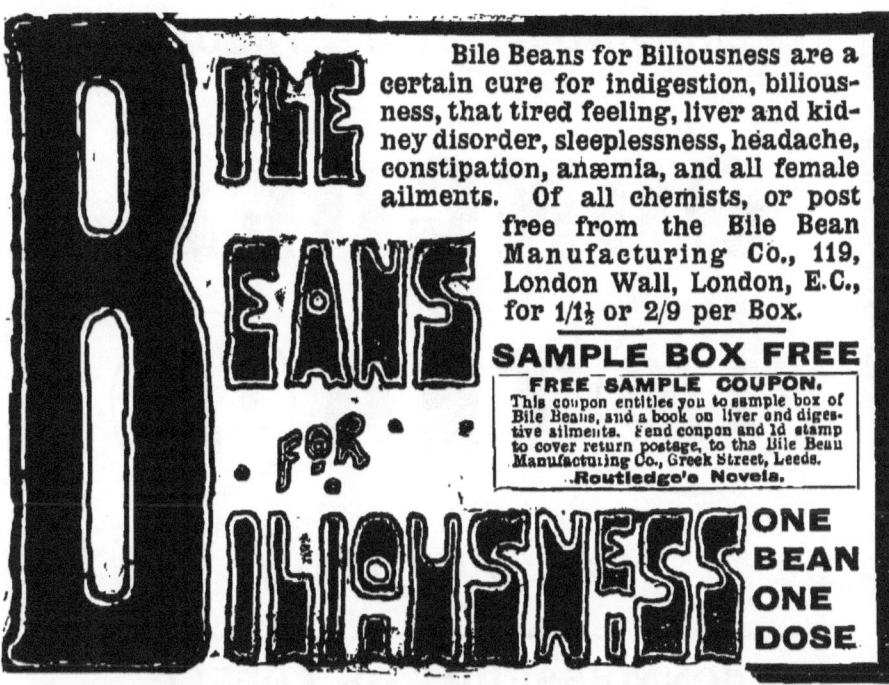

ENGLAND'S BEST VALUE!

BONGOLA

(1/6) TEA (1/9)

HAS <u>NO</u> EQUAL!

CONNOISSEURS OF <u>COFFEE</u>

DRINK THE

RED
WHITE
& BLUE

Delicious for Breakfast and after Dinner.

In making, use <u>less quantity</u>, it being so much stronger
than ordinary <u>Coffee</u>.

STANDARD NOVELS.

Strongly bound in Cloth, price 2s. each.

Ainsworth, W. H.—

The Windsor Edition, in 21 vols.

Miser's Daughter
St. James's
Flitch of Bacon
Guy Fawkes
Crichton
Spendthrift
Boscobel
Ovingdean Grange
Mervyn Clitheroe
Auriol
Preston Fight
Stanley Brereton
Beau Nash
Jack Sheppard
The Lancashire Witches
The Manchester Rebels
Old St. Paul's
Rookwood
The Star Chamber
Windsor Castle
The Tower of London

Austen, Jane.—

Pride and Prejudice
Sense and Sensibility
Mansfield Park
Emma

Bronte, Charlotte, Emily and Jane.—

Jane Eyre
Shirley
Wuthering Heights
Villette

Carleton, William.—

Willy Reilly

Cockton, Henry.—

Sylvester Sound
Stanley Thorn

Collins, Wilkie.—

Antonina

Cooper, Fenimore.—

The Deerslayer
The Pathfinder
The Last of the Mohicans
The Pioneers
The Prairie
The Red Rover
The Pilot
The Two Admirals
The Waterwitch
The Spy
The Sea Lions
Miles Wallingford

STANDARD NOVELS—*continued.*

Cooper, Fenimore—*continued.*

Lionel Lincoln
The Headsman
Homeward Bound
The Crater ; or, Vulcan's
    Peak
Wing and Wing
Jack Tier
Satanstoe
The Red Skins
The Heidenmauer
Precaution
The Monikins
The Ways of the Hour
Mercedes
Afloat and Ashore
Home as Found
    (Sequel to " Homeward Bound ")
Oak Openings

Cooper, Thomas.—

The Family Feud

Crowe, Mrs.—

The Nightside of Nature

Croly, Dr.—

Salathiel

Dickens, Charles.—

Barnaby Rudge
Old Curiosity Shop
Dombey and Son

Dickens, Charles—*continued.*

Grimaldi the Clown
    With Cruikshank's illustrations
Martin Chuzzlewit
Pickwick Papers
Pictures from Italy and
    American Notes
Bleak House

Du Boisgobey, Fortune.—

The Bride of a Day
The Half-Sister's Secret
Married for Love

Dumas, Alexandre.—

*The Fleur-de-lis Edition, in
15 vols.*

The Three Musketeers
Monte Cristo
Forty-five Guardsmen
Taking the Bastile
The Queen's Necklace
The Conspirators
The Regent's Daughter
Memoirs of a Physician
The Countess de Charny
The Vicomte de Brage-
    lonne. *Vol.* 1
The Vicomte de Brage-
    lonne. *Vol.* 2
Chevalier de Maison Rouge
Chicot the Jester
Marguerite de Valois
Twenty   s After

STANDARD NOVELS—*continued.*

Ferrier, Miss.—

Marriage
The Inheritance
Destiny

Fielding, Henry.—

Tom Jones
Joseph Andrews
Amelia

Gaskell, Mrs.—

Mary Barton

Grant, James.—

The Aide-de-Camp Edition. To be completed in 56 vols.

The Aide de Camp
The Scottish Cavalier
Jane Seton
The Yellow Frigate
The Romance of War
Oliver Ellis
Mary of Lorraine
Lucy Arden
Colville of the Guards
The Constable of France
Did She Love Him ?
The Duke of Albany's Highlanders
Dulcie Carlyon
First Love and Last Love
The Lord Hermitage
Philip Rollo

Haliburton, Judge.—

The Clockmaker
The Attaché

Hugo, Victor.—

History of a Crime
Ninety-Three
Toilers of the Sea
By Order of the King

Kingsley, Charles.—

Yeast
Hypatia

Lever, Charles.—

Harry Lorrequer
Jack Hinton
Arthur O'Leary
Con Cregan
Tom Burke

Lover, Samuel.—

Handy Andy

Lytton, Lord.—

The Stevenage Edition, in 28 vols.

Author's Copyright Editions, containing Prefaces to be found in no other Editions.

Pelham
Paul Clifford
Rienzi
Ernest Maltravers

STANDARD NOVELS—*continued.*

Lytton, Lord—*continued.*

Alice ; or, The Mysteries
Disowned
Devereux
Godolphin
Leila ; Pilgrims of the Rhine
Falkland ; Zicci
Zanoni
Harold
Lucretia
The Coming Race
Kenelm Chillingly
Pausanias: and The Haunted
    and the Haunters
My Novel.   *Vol.* 1
    ,,   *Vol.* 2
What will He do with It ?
           Vol. 1
    ,,   *Vol.* 2
The Parisians.   *Vol.* 1
    ,,   *Vol.* 2
The Caxtons
Eugene Aram
Last Days of Pompeii
The Last of the Barons
Night and Morning
A Strange Story

Marryat, Captain.—

Frank Mildmay
Phantom Ship
Peter Simple
The King's Own
Newton Forster
Jacob Faithful

Marryat, Captain—*continued.*

Dog Fiend
The Poacher
Percival Keene
Rattlin, the Reefer.
    Edited by CAPTAIN MARRYAT.
Valerie
Olla Podrida

Maxwell, W. H.—

The Bivouac

Mayhew, The Brothers.—

The Greatest Plague of Life

Miller, Thomas.—

Gideon Giles

Mounteney-Jephson, R.—

Tom Bullkley
The Roll of the Drum
The Red Rag

Poe, Edgar Allan.—

The Gold-Bug, and other
    Tales
Landor's Cottage, and other
    Tales

Porter, Jane.—

The Pastor's Fireside
Thaddeus of Warsaw